BY FANNIE FLAGG

THE
WONDER
BOY
OF
WHISTLE
STOP

THE
WONDER
BOY
OF
WHISTLE
STOP

A NOVEL

Fannie Flagg

RANDOM HOUSE

NEW YORK

The Wonder Boy of Whistle Stop is a work of fiction. Names, characters, places, and incidents are the products of the author's imagination or are used fictitiously. Any resemblance to actual events, locales, or persons, living or dead, is entirely coincidental.

Copyright © 2020 by Willina Lane Productions, Inc.

All rights reserved.

Published in the United States by Random House, an imprint and division of Penguin Random House LLC, New York.

RANDOM HOUSE and the HOUSE colophon are registered trademarks of Penguin Random House LLC.

Hardback ISBN 9780593133842
Ebook ISBN 9780593133859

Printed in the United States of America on acid-free paper

randomhousebooks.com

2 4 6 8 9 7 5 3 1

First Edition

Book design by Victoria Wong

For Colleen

THE
WONDER
BOY
OF
WHISTLE
STOP

Prologue

L & N TERMINAL TRAIN STATION
BIRMINGHAM, ALABAMA
November 29, 1938, 8:10 A.M.

IT WAS A cool November morning. Inside the large train station, shards of clear bright sunlight shot down through the glass ceiling as arriving and departing passengers and porters with carts piled high with luggage hurried back and forth across the white marble floor in a beehive of activity. Sounds of happy chatter and trains pulling in and out of the station echoed throughout the entire building.

Over on platform 7, the Crescent, the long silver train from New Orleans, was now ready to receive its Birmingham passengers, and Mr. and Mrs. Arthur J. Hornbeck quickly climbed aboard, headed to New York City for their annual Christmas shopping trip.

Mrs. Hornbeck, carrying six large round hatboxes, three in each hand, happily banged down the aisle, hitting several sleeping passengers in the head as she passed by. Mr. Hornbeck, with his newspaper tucked under his arm, followed five steps behind.

Some twelve and half minutes later, after all the hatboxes had been stacked and her fur coat carefully hung up in the compartment closet, Mrs. Hornbeck was finally ready to settle down, relax, and enjoy the ride. She looked out the window just as they were approaching the Whistle Stop, Alabama, railroad crossing. As they got closer, she suddenly noticed a little blond boy in faded overalls standing by the tracks, smiling and waving at the train as it went by. Mrs. Hornbeck had a little boy at home about his age, so as they rode past him, she smiled and waved. When the little boy saw her, he began running under her window, waving back at her, as hard and for as long as he could. She watched him until he and the little dog running along beside him became smaller and smaller, until they were both completely out of sight.

After a long moment, Mrs. Hornbeck turned to her husband with a concerned look on her face and said, "Arthur, I think that little boy back there had an arm missing."

Never looking up from his paper, he replied, "Well, I'll be."

Mrs. Hornbeck sighed, sat back in her seat, and began fingering her triple strand of pearls, then said, "Oh, what a shame. He couldn't have been more than seven or eight at the most, and he was the cutest little thing. You should have seen him. So happy, smiling away. . . . Well, bless his precious little heart. My cousin Charles had a little finger missing, but an entire arm? I wonder what in the world could have happened to him."

Her husband glanced over at her. "What did you say?"

"I said, I wonder how that poor little boy lost his arm. What could have happened?"

Mr. Hornbeck, a master at stating the obvious, replied, "Well . . . something must have."

SHE HAD SEEN the little boy for only a few seconds at the most. But every year after that, as their train passed through the Whistle Stop crossing, Mrs. Hornbeck always leaned forward in her seat and looked out, hoping to see him again. And every year when he was not there, she would always turn and ask her husband, "Arthur, I wonder whatever became of that cute little blond boy with the one arm."

"Beats me," he always said.

Sheriff Grady Kilgore

GRADY KILGORE, A big barrel-chested bear of a man in his seventies, had been the sheriff of Whistle Stop, Alabama, until 1958, when he and his wife, Gladys, had moved to Tennessee. Today, Grady had driven down to Whistle Stop from Nashville with his grandson and was standing on the railroad tracks, looking across the street to where the old Whistle Stop Cafe used to be. Kudzu vines had grown all over the buildings and had covered most of the block. It was hard for his grandson to tell what was underneath.

Grady pointed over to one of the buildings. "That's the old post office that Dot Weems ran, and right there's the cafe, next to Opal Butts's beauty shop, where your grandma got her hair done up every Saturday morning." Grady stood there looking around and was sad to see how much the place had changed since the last time he'd stopped by.

By now, the old two-lane highway from Birmingham to Whistle Stop had been bypassed by a new six-lane interstate, and most of the area was now just a dumping ground. Old rusty cars and trucks had been abandoned by the tracks, left to slowly fall apart. Empty beer cans and whiskey bottles were everywhere. And as a sad sign of the times, Grady noticed there was a lot of drug paraphernalia scattered around that hadn't been there before.

The Baptist church, where he had heard Reverend Scroggins preach every Sunday, was now almost falling down, the stained-glass windows broken, the pews removed and sold. All that was left of the town were some of the old buildings and the old Threadgoode home, and that was barely standing. Vandals had pretty much destroyed everything else. Grady turned to his grandson and shook his head. "When I get to thinkin' how this place used to be, and what it is now, it just makes me sick. It wasn't never a fancy town, but it was clean. Now there's junk scattered everywhere. And the old Threadgoode house is full of graffiti, the windows all knocked out. You'd never know to look at it now, but that house used to be the prettiest one in town. For the life of me, I still cain't figure out why Whistle Stop went to seed like it did. I even heard the whole town was sold, and they were gonna knock it all down and build a tire factory out here."

Grady looked across the street again and sighed. "I don't know why they're just lettin' the old cafe sit and rot away like that. It just don't seem right. That cafe used to be like going to a good friend's house to eat. Two great gals ran it. Idgie Threadgoode and Ruth Jamison. You woulda loved 'em. Everybody in town used to eat there, all the railroad men and their families. Every Christmas Day their cook, Sipsey, and the gals would lay out a big spread, and we'd all go over and eat, open our presents, and sing carols." Then, unexpectedly, Grady let out a little sob. He quickly turned away, pulled out a handkerchief, and blew his nose and looked apologetic.

"Sorry about that. Oh Lordy. I don't need to go thinkin' about the old days . . . but lots of good times were had in that old cafe with Ruth and Idgie. Ruth's son, little Buddy, grew up in that cafe. Poor kid. Lost his arm when he wasn't much older than you." Grady then carefully folded his handkerchief and put it back into his pocket.

Then he said, "Now, you may not believe this, but a few years back on Christmas Day your grandma and me was over in Birmingham visiting Opal Butts, and while they were busy cooking up dinner, I snuck out and took a little ride out here. And I was standing right here, on this same spot we are now, when—real quiet like at first—I started to hear a piano playing and people laughing, and it was coming from over there, right where the cafe used to be. I looked around and there wasn't nobody there, but I swear I heard it. What do you think it could have been?"

His grandson rubbed his hands together and said, "I don't know, Granddaddy, but can we go now? I'm getting cold."

Dot Weems

DOT WEEMS WAS a friendly little woman who just loved to chat. When she was younger, she had hoped for a literary career on the order of her idol, Edna Ferber. But at seventeen, she had fallen in love with "the man of her dreams," and had married Wilbur Weems instead.

Later she would often joke that even if she hadn't become a famous novelist, she was still "a woman of letters." Aside from single-handedly running the Whistle Stop Post Office for sixteen years, Dot also wrote and published a weekly newsletter reporting on all the town's activities under a banner that read:

The Weems Weekly
(WHISTLE STOP, ALABAMA'S WEEKLY BULLETIN)
"No gossip, just the plain facts, folks!"

Dot had just sent out the week's newsletter, and this morning people all over Whistle Stop were busy reading it.

The Weems Weekly
(WHISTLE STOP, ALABAMA'S WEEKLY BULLETIN)
November 30, 1935

The Turkey Thief

Hi Gang. Well, I hope you all had a happy Thanksgiving. I know for sure that Wilbur's old hound dog, Cooter, did. Yes, that was him you saw running through town Thanksgiving Day with my freshly cooked turkey in his mouth. The one he had just snatched off the table, the minute my back was turned, trailing my stuffing all through the living room. Honestly, men and their dogs! Thank heavens my next-door neighbor, Ninny Threadgoode, took pity on us and had us over for dinner or Wilbur and I would have gone turkeyless! And not only was Ninny's turkey delicious, we also enjoyed Sipsey's sweet potato pie that Idgie sent over from the cafe. So as Mr. Shakespeare says, "All's well that ends well." Yum yum.

But now to the important news: It seems we have a rare archaeological find right here in Whistle Stop! Where? According to Idgie Threadgoode, right in our very own backyard! Well, the backyard of the cafe, that is. Idgie reports that she and little Buddy were out in the back digging up red worms to go fishing with, when she dug up (hold on to your hats, folks) a five-million-year-old dinosaur tooth! Idgie has it out on display on the counter at the cafe for all to see, so if you want to take a look, go on over.

Good news from the beauty shop: I am also happy to announce that Opal Butts says she finally got the hair dryer to working again, so if you missed last week's hair appointment, she will be working overtime to fit you in. I know the ladies who are going to the Elks Club dinner Saturday night will be happy to hear it. Me, too.

More good news: Sheriff Grady said that other than a

few minor mishaps, involving a few of our citizens and too much "Old Man Whiskey," we have been crime free for another year. Thank you, Grady.

Your faithful scribe,

. . . Dot Weems . . .

P.S. Don't forget to tell the kids to get their letters to Santa Claus written. Remind them that it's a long way to the North Pole from Whistle Stop, and Santa needs plenty of time to make all those toys.

LATER THAT NIGHT, Wilbur Weems, a tall, thin man, was laughing when he came home for supper. As he walked in the door, he said, "Well, Dot, thanks to you, everybody in town was over at the cafe today to see that darned dinosaur tooth."

Dot was putting a bowl of mashed potatoes down by his plate. "I know. I went over myself. Do you think it's real?"

Wilbur sat down and took a swig of iced tea. "Knowing Idgie, I doubt it. She just loves to pull jokes. Remember that petrified two-headed frog she had in a jar last year? I found out later it was rubber."

"No, you don't mean it."

"Oh yeah. She told me she bought it over in Birmingham at the magic shop."

"Oh my," Dot said as she sat down and passed him the cornbread. "What will that girl come up with next?"

"Who knows? But *whatever* it is, it will be fun, you can count on that."

Idgie Threadgoode

JUST LIKE EVERYBODY else in town, Dot and Wilbur Weems had known and loved Idgie Threadgoode all her life. Idgie had always been a tomboy, always tall for her age, with short, curly blond hair. From the time she could walk, she'd loved to play sports with the boys and climb trees. Most of the time, she was up in the big chinaberry tree in the front yard of the Threadgoode house or else sitting up on the roof. Her mother said she must be related to a monkey, because Idgie would and could climb anything.

When she was around six, she had been playing over at the rail yard, and that afternoon, when her mother was out sweeping the front porch, she happened to look up as the five o'clock to Atlanta was passing the Threadgoode house, and there sat Idgie on the top of the train waving at her mother as she rode by.

Of course, her mother was hysterical, thinking Idgie was going to fall off and be killed any minute. But luckily they were able to telegraph ahead to the next station, and got her down over at Pell City, safe and sound. Growing up, both Idgie and her younger brother, Julian, had idolized their older brother Buddy. He was the one who had taught Idgie to shoot and fish and play football and baseball. And if anyone dared Idgie to do something, she usually did it. Everyone always said she was very brave for a girl.

One time at school, when a boy had thrown a snake into the

girls' bathroom, girls were running everywhere, screaming at the top of their lungs. Everybody but Idgie. She had grabbed the snake and chased that boy across the field, caught him, and stuffed it down his shirt. Reverend Scroggins, the Baptist preacher, heard about the skirmish, and his sermon that Sunday had been Psalm 133:1: "How Very Good and Pleasant It Is When Kindred Live Together in Unity."

But Idgie hadn't heard the sermon. As usual on Sunday mornings, she was down at the Warrior River with her brother Buddy, fishing for catfish.

Idgie had always been a little wild at heart, a little restless, but after her big brother Buddy was killed in a train accident, she became even more so. She started spending time down at the River Club, running with a rough bunch, drinking and playing poker in the back room. And nobody could do a thing with her. Not until twenty-one-year-old Ruth Jamison came to Whistle Stop that summer to teach Bible school. For some reason Idgie behaved around Ruth. Her mother said that if Ruth had not come along when she did, she didn't know what would have become of Idgie. But after Ruth left to go home to Georgia and get married, Idgie reverted back to her old ways.

But then a few years later, when Ruth left her husband and came back to live in Whistle Stop, Idgie's father gave her five hundred dollars to start a business. So Idgie bought the cafe, and she and Ruth ran it. Momma and Poppa Threadgoode hoped it would help settle Idgie down. And it had. Most of the time. Although, being Idgie, she had still done a few things she shouldn't have. Things that Ruth didn't know about.

Buddy Jr.

THE YEAR RUTH'S little boy was born, he was legally adopted by the Threadgoode family. Ruth had named him Buddy Jr. after the son the Threadgoodes had lost. Momma and Poppa Threadgoode and Idgie's brothers Cleo and Julian had all stepped in and helped raise him.

Ninny Threadgoode, a sweet lady who was married to Idgie's brother Cleo, lived just up the street from the cafe. At present, she had a cat who had just given birth to eight kittens. Every day, ten-year-old Buddy would go over to Ninny's house and play with them for hours. Buddy loved spending time with his Aunt Ninny, and she loved having his company.

One afternoon, when Ninny was over at the cafe visiting with Ruth, she said, "That boy of yours is a real wonder boy."

Ruth smiled. "Why do you say that?"

Ninny laughed. "Because he's always a wonderin' about somethin' or another. Why do kittens purr, or why do rabbits have long ears? This morning, when he was over at my house, he says to me, 'Aunt Ninny, I wonder why chickens have feathers and wings, but they don't fly off anywhere?' So I said, 'That's a good question, honey. If I was a chicken and I saw Sipsey headed toward me with her five-pound skillet, I'd sure fly away if I could.'"

Ninny was right about Buddy. Every train that would pass by, he would wonder who was on it. Where were they going? And what were they going to do when they got there?

Of course, Idgie took all his wondering as a sign that Buddy was a genius and was going to do great things one day. And she never quit believing it.

Even after Buddy lost his arm playing over by the railroad tracks, Idgie was determined to keep him doing all the things he had done before. Today they were down at the lake fishing. Buddy stood there on the bank staring across the lake, and then said, "Hey, Aunt Idgie, should I send Peggy Hadley a valentine?"

"Well, why wouldn't you? You like her, don't you?"

"Yes ma'am."

"Then sure, you should."

After a moment he said, "Yeah . . . but I wonder if she likes me."

Idgie looked at him. "Well, of course she likes you, Buddy. You? The smartest and handsomest boy in the whole world? Who wouldn't? Besides, she told me she did."

"She did?"

"Yep . . . but don't tell her I told you."

Buddy smiled, and then a few minutes later said, "Hey, Aunt Idgie, I wonder why catfish have whiskers."

"I don't know, honey, but I think there might be one biting on your line right now."

Buddy's eyes grew big. "Whoa!" After a struggle he pulled in his fish. "Wow . . . look at him, Aunt Idgie. I wonder how much he weighs."

"Oh, I'd say at least twenty pounds."

"Do you think so?"

"No, but let's tell your mother that, okay?"

"Okay."

Buddy loved his mother, but Aunt Idgie was his best friend—

the one who played football and baseball with him. The one who always took him on adventures.

Just last month, Idgie had read in the *Farmers' Almanac* that there was to be a huge meteor shower the following Tuesday. That night, they were sitting on the back steps watching all the falling stars streaking across the sky, when Idgie suddenly pulled out her baseball glove, jumped up, and ran out in the yard. After a long moment, she yelled out, "I caught one!" and then ran back and handed it to Buddy.

"Look, Buddy, I've caught you a lucky star. You know what that means, don't ya? You've got a lot of good luck coming your way, kiddo."

Of course, it was just a rock she had scooped up off the ground, but Buddy was delighted with it. And he couldn't wait to find out what good luck the future would bring.

Twenty-Five Years Later

FAIRHOPE, ALABAMA
December 21, 1964

AT ONE TIME Whistle Stop had been a bustling little railroad town, ten miles from Birmingham, employing over two hundred railroad workers. But as passenger train travel slowly declined, and the big railroad switching yard shut down and moved, people started to find jobs elsewhere, and the town's population declined too. With so many people leaving, Dot's weekly newsletters became smaller as the weeks and months went by. People in Whistle Stop tried to hang on as long as they could, but the real beginning of the end was when Idgie Threadgoode suddenly closed down the cafe and moved to Florida. For weeks afterward, old men and little boys kept peeking through the wooden slats on the cafe window, hoping it wasn't true. But it was. And with the beauty shop and the cafe gone, and then later, when the U.S. Post Office disbanded their Whistle Stop office, what had once been a busy street and the hub of the community was now just one long, empty block. With no real town left, the ones who stayed found themselves stranded out in the country, in the middle of nowhere, with no jobs or places to shop. Eventually, even some of the old diehards like Dot and Wilbur Weems were finally forced to accept the inevitable and leave.

Dot and Wilbur Weems were now living in the little town of Fairhope in south Alabama in a small white house across the street from the Mobile Bay. Dot liked where they had moved, but she still missed her old friends and neighbors from Whistle Stop, all the people that she had grown up with, or the ones she had watched grow up. And even though most had moved somewhere else, Dot had stayed in touch with them. And they had all stayed in touch with her, either by phone or letter, keeping her informed of what they had been up to.

Although she no longer published *The Weems Weekly*, Dot began to send a Christmas letter each year, to try to keep the old Whistle Stop community connected.

And so as usual at this time of year, Dot was sitting with a pencil behind her ear at her kitchen table, piled with stacks of papers, letters, photos, erasers, and notebooks. She had cleared out a spot for her old Royal typewriter and placed it in the middle of the mess. She was just about to start writing when her husband, Wilbur, wearing a brown-checked bathrobe, floated through, poured himself a cup of coffee, and then floated back out. He knew not to talk to her when she was working. As soon as he left, she began typing.

CHRISTMAS 1964

Well, gang,

Believe it or not, another year has come and almost gone. And I ask you, is it just me, or is December the twenty-fifth coming around sooner than it used to? Wasn't it just the Fourth of July a week ago? Christmas slipped up on me so fast this year, I barely had time to get all my notes together, but here goes.

News from My Home Front: I am pleased to report that after his fall off the back porch, Wilbur is finally off his walker, and as of this writing not yet "off his rocker." He says to tell you all hello from him. We so appreciated all the get-well cards and letters you sent him. They sure helped cheer the grumpy old guy up.

As usual, Idgie Threadgoode has gotten our holiday season off to a good start with the arrival of her jars of homemade honey and a big box of oranges from Florida. Idgie says the sun is shining and business is good! She also says her brother Julian is now sporting a brand-new set of teeth and is busy smiling at everyone he sees.

Gladys Kilgore wrote us from Tennessee, and says that Sheriff Grady Kilgore is finally retiring in May, and they plan a trip to Florida to visit Julian and Idgie, and maybe a stop by here on the way back. Here's hoping.

On a sad note: So sorry to report that Ninny and Cleo Threadgoode's son, Albert, left us this year. Never met a sweeter boy. I am also sorry to report that Jessie Ray Scroggins's wife has filed for divorce, again. Too bad. Hopefully they will work it out. Just had word that Sipsey Peavey is not doing well and is now living with her son, Big George, and his wife, Onzell. Sipsey turns ninety-eight on February 11, so be sure and send a card if you can. How many years did Sipsey work at the cafe with Idgie and Ruth? At least twenty-five. And what would you give to have a plate of Sipsey's fried green tomatoes? I'd give a million, if I had it.

News Flash: Opal Butts has moved her beauty shop again, so write her at her new address in Birmingham, c/o The Capri Apartments, 2012 Highland Ave. Opal says it's a brand-new swinging singles complex, and although she is no spring chicken, she is still having a lot of fun. I am also pleased to report that her daughter, Jewel Ann, is following in her mother's footsteps and is attending beauty school. Opal says that Jewel plans to specialize in body waves and eyebrow shaping. Never heard of eyebrow shaping, but it must be the latest thing. I myself am still doing pin curls, and letting my eyebrows do what they want to.

Gosh dang it all, gang, I don't know why, but this year Christmas is making me just a little homesick. Do any of you remember all the wonderful Christmases we used to spend at the cafe, the whole town showing up, cats and dogs included? Sheriff Grady all dressed up as Santa Claus, handing out all the presents? And all the big red shiny balls Idgie hung on that old deer head over the counter? I have so many sweet memories of those days. Remember little Buddy Threadgoode's special Christmas gift that one year? I do. Who could ever forget the look on his little face?

Of course I'm glad I'm alive now, but sometimes don't you wish you could just take a magic carpet ride back and relive some of the good old times in Whistle Stop? Are any of you old enough to remember when Idgie Thread-goode was seven years old, and marched in the Fourth of July parade dressed up as Uncle Sam? Never saw a cuter Uncle Sam or prouder parents than Momma and Poppa Threadgoode that day. Or remember the Dill Pickle Club, of which my other half and Idgie were members, and all the mischief they used to pull? Who do you think put the nanny goat on top of Reverend Scroggins's house? I don't know for sure but I can guess it was Idgie and her pals. And the "womanless wedding" the club put on for charity, when six-foot-four Sheriff Grady came prissing down the aisle dressed as the lovely bride? Oh my, those are just a few memories of mine. I sure would appreciate your sending me some of your favorite memories of Whistle Stop for next year's letter.

You all know I like to close on a happy note, and oh boy do I have one this year! On November 9, Buddy and Peggy Threadgoode welcomed a brand-new baby daughter. They've named her Norma Ruth, and I know her great aunt Idgie is still jumping up and down over the good news. We just wish Buddy's mother, Ruth Jamison, could have lived to meet her new little namesake granddaughter. Buddy is still stationed in Germany, serving as a veterinarian in the U.S. Army K-9 Corps, but Peggy says they hope to return stateside within the year. She also writes that the latest artificial arm the army has outfitted Bud with is the best one yet. He'll sure need two good ones to hold new baby Ruthie. She weighed in at almost eight pounds.

It's still hard for me to believe that the same two little kids we used to see running barefooted around Whistle Stop are all grown up now with a baby of their own. Oh well, as they say. Semper fidelis.

I'll sign off for this year, but do come and see us if you can. We live right across the street from the Mobile Bay, and as Wilbur says, "Drop in sometime." Ha. Ha. Some joke. Men!

So until next year, Merry Christmas, and Happy New Year!

Your faithful scribe,
Dot

Dot pulled her letter out of the typewriter, and a few seconds later Wilbur, who had been waiting, knocked lightly on the kitchen door. "Are you done?"

"Yes, I think so. Come on in."

Wilbur, who was dressed and ready to take the letter up to the mimeograph machine at the print shop, walked in, and she handed it to him to read. As usual, Dot was anxious to hear his feedback. As he was still reading she asked, "Well . . . what do you think?"

He nodded and smiled. "I think it's great. But, hon, I think you meant to say 'tempus' here, not 'semper fidelis.'"

"Doesn't that mean 'time flies'?"

"No, 'semper fidelis' is the Marine Corps motto."

"Ooh. That's right. I don't know where my mind is this morning. Thank you very muchly, for catching that."

"You're welcome very muchly."

"What would I do without you?"

"I've asked myself that question all my life."

Welcome to the World

A FEW MONTHS after Idgie Threadgoode had moved to Florida, and with a little help from her brother Julian, she'd opened a brand-new business called the Bee Happy Fresh Honey and Fruit Stand. It was only a wooden shed, but since it sat on the side of a well-traveled road, it did very well.

It was early November, and Bud and Peggy Threadgoode had promised to let Idgie know the minute the baby was born. The time was getting close, and an anxious Idgie had spent days running back and forth from the fruit stand to her house, waiting for word, when the telegram finally came.

She quickly tore it open and read it, and then ran out on the screen porch and yelled at Julian, who lived next door. "Julian! Whoopee! It's a girl, and they named her after Ruth. Mother and baby both doing fine! Whoopee!" She was so excited that she ran back in the house and sat down and started a letter.

P.O. Box 346
Kissimmee, Florida

Dear Little Miss Ruth Threadgoode,
I've just heard that you entered the world today at seven pounds and nine ounces. Well done! And a great big wel-

come to the world to you! Oh, what fun you are going to
have growing up with that silly daddy of yours, and with so
much love from your mother, Peggy. I am so pleased they
named you after your grandmother Ruth. Just so you know,
Ruth Jamison was the most wonderful person in the world
and I know she would be so proud, too. Your daddy says you
look just like her, with your big brown eyes, and that you
are as pretty as a picture.

I don't know what to buy a little baby, so until I can fig-
ure it out, I am sending all my best to you, and your
momma and daddy. Uncle Julian does the same.

Love,
Your Aunt Idgie

P.S. When you get old enough to travel, come and see
an old lady sometime, will you?

Idgie put the letter in the mailbox, and was still smiling as she
walked back to the house. Wow. There was now a new little Ruth
in the world. The thought made her so happy she didn't know
what to do. She grabbed a candy bar from the kitchen and went
out and sat on the porch, enjoying her candy and thinking about
the future. The baby was not even a day old yet and Idgie was already planning all the fun things they could do together, when an
image from the past suddenly crossed her mind. It was of a day in
spring and Ruth Jamison was sitting across a meadow smiling at
her, looking so young and beautiful. Then it occurred to Idgie
that if that same young girl was alive today, she would now be a
grandmother. How could that be? Idgie tried her best to envision
Ruth as an older woman with wrinkles and gray hair, but as hard
as she tried she just couldn't do it. In her mind Ruth would always

remain young and beautiful. She would always remember her just that way.

Idgie had often thought that if she had somehow had the power to stop time, she would have stopped it when they both were young. But then, if she had, there would have been no Buddy in the world, or his new little baby. As heartbreaking as it could be at times, maybe life knew best. Idgie didn't know the answer. She had finally stopped trying to figure it out and had accepted the fact that life was a mystery, yet to be solved by people much smarter than she was. All she knew was that a little bit of Ruth was still alive, and she just couldn't wait to meet her.

U.S. Army Base

BAUMHOLDER, GERMANY
December 31, 1964

IT WAS FIVE degrees outside and snowing when Peggy Thread-goode, a redhead with freckles, walked in the door with the mail from the PX and called out "Hey, Bud, we just got Dot's Christmas letter."

A tall blond man with brown eyes looked up from the medical chart he was studying. "Oh, great. How are they doing?"

"I don't know yet." After she'd hung up her hat and coat, Peggy came in and sat down beside him, opened the letter, and started reading.

After a moment she said, "They're doing fine. They still seem to like it down there in Fairhope. She says she got Idgie's honey and oranges from Florida. . . . Jessie Ray Scroggins is getting divorced again."

"Oh, too bad. Poor guy."

"Well, I'm not surprised. You know his daddy has got to be upset, poor Reverend Scroggins. And let's see . . . ah, here it is. She announced that we had a baby and named her after your mother. And says she bets Idgie is happy about that."

Bud smiled. "That's nice."

Peggy laughed. "Then she says that she and Wilbur remember us when we were just kids, running around town barefooted."

Bud sat back in his chair and crossed his arms. "Good old Dot and Wilbur. I miss the heck out of 'em, don't you?"

Peggy nodded. "Yeah, I do. And she also mentions your new arm, and says she misses Christmas at the cafe, and all the fun we used to have. And she also asks if people could send her some of their happiest memories of Whistle Stop." Peggy looked at Bud.

"That's a hard one, we have so many."

"Not really. I sure know what mine would be."

"What?"

Bud smiled a wicked little smile. "A certain night out at Double Springs Lake."

Peggy was alarmed and started to blush. "Bud Threadgoode, you're not going to write and tell her that!"

He laughed. "No, but it's quite a memory, you have to admit."

Just then baby Ruthie woke up from her nap and started crying. Bud ran over to the crib and picked her up. Peggy laughed and said, "You're going to spoil that baby something awful."

"I don't care. She should be spoiled," he said, as he walked around the room, cooing at her. "Good morning, my beautiful little Ruthie. Your daddy loves you, yes he does."

Peggy shook her head. "Lord, Bud, you would think there had never been another baby born in the entire world."

"Well, there hasn't. Not like this little girl," he said, rocking her back and forth. "She's special. Aren't you, sweetheart?"

Peggy walked over and held out her arms. "She may be special, but I need to change her diaper."

"Oh." Bud reluctantly handed over the baby.

The truth was, they were both madly in love with little Ruthie. After having waited so long to start a family, they were over the moon with joy. Bud in particular. He had wished for a little girl and he'd gotten one.

Dot Weems

FAIRHOPE, ALABAMA

Christmas 1970

Well, folks, another year and we're still here, alive and kicking. I am anyway. Wilbur dropped a hammer on his foot and broke his toe, so he's not doing much kicking these days. But I am happy to report that he finally went and got some hearing aids, so I don't have to shout anymore. You try playing bingo with a deaf man.

And now to the news of the day, as they say.

Received a darling photo of Bud, Peggy, and little Ruthie. I can't believe how much Ruthie has grown since last year. This new one was taken of the three of them standing in front of her daddy's brand-new Threadgoode Animal Clinic building in Silver Spring, Maryland, where they are now living. I must say it's good to have them back home in the old USA. It looks like a very nice building and we're so happy to see the Threadgoode name on it. Our Bud has done very well for himself, and we are all proud of him.

And speaking of Threadgoodes, my old friend and former neighbor Ninny Threadgoode sent me another one of her favorite Whistle Stop memories. She says she remembers Saturday mornings when Idgie used to pile all the kids in Whistle Stop into that old car of hers and drive them over to Birmingham to the movies and treat them all to popcorn and a coke. She said nobody loved kids more than Idgie. I agree.

Sad news: Grady Kilgore, who was in Birmingham over Thanksgiving, took a ride over to Whistle Stop and reports that someone must have stolen the old Whistle Stop railroad crossing sign, because it's not there anymore. Reverend Scroggins wrote to tell us that his son Jessie Ray just got back from the service and has wrecked another car. That makes three so far.

On a happier note: Our old pal Opal Butts said she ran into Sipsey's granddaughter Alberta, who is now living in Birmingham, and says that she is attending a fancy cooking school and hopes to become a chef. Good for her! Maybe she will become the next Julia Child.

Merry Christmas, gang!

Your faithful scribe,
Dot

P.S. We don't get out to the movies much anymore. Write and tell us some good shows to look at. Wilbur and I like *Carol Burnett, Candid Camera,* and *What's My Line?* How about you?

The Visit

RIGHT AFTER IDGIE opened her new fruit and honey stand, somebody called her in Florida and made her a good offer. So Idgie sold the cafe over the phone. She only made a few hundred dollars, but it was just enough to buy the little pink stucco house right next to her brother Julian's. It had a big screened-in porch with a white metal swan on the door that Idgie loved.

Ruthie Threadgoode had heard a lot about her dad's Aunt Idgie, and she received a birthday card from her every year, but she had never met her. When Ruthie turned six, Idgie sent her a picture of herself taken at an ostrich farm, sitting on an ostrich. She'd signed it *Happy birthday from two old birds.*

One month before Ruthie's seventh birthday, Bud said to Peggy, "Honey, do you think we could take a week or so off? Take a trip? I'd love to go down to Florida and see Aunt Idgie. She's been dying to meet Ruthie, and it's been way too long since we've seen her. And Ruthie needs to meet her Aunt Idgie, don't you think?"

Peggy said, "Absolutely, I do."

So plans were made, bags were packed, and the three of them headed down to Florida. When Idgie heard they were coming she was so excited she danced a little jig. By the time they got there, everybody in town and thereabouts, even strangers passing through, knew that Idgie's little niece was coming down from Maryland to visit.

THE DAY THEY arrived, Idgie and Julian were sitting in Idgie's front yard waiting, both tanned from the Florida sun. Bud was glad to see that although Aunt Idgie had a few more wrinkles, and her short, curly blond hair was now snow-white, when she smiled, her sparkly blue eyes were still full of spirit, still full of the devil.

When all the hugs and hellos were over, Idgie looked at Ruthie and said, "Well, now, if you're not the spittin' image of your grandmother Ruth, I don't know who is." Idgie winked at Bud and then looked at her again. "Ruthie, your daddy may have been the cutest baby in the world, but I can tell you for a fact, you take the prize. You are the most beautiful little girl in the world, hands down. I think you deserve a bowl of ice cream, don't you?"

Ruthie giggled. "Yes ma'am."

"Well, come on in. Your room's ready and ice cream is a-waiting."

After they'd unpacked and Ruthie had opened a present Idgie had for her, they all sat out on the porch, talking and drinking iced tea. Then Idgie said, "I'll be right back," and got up and went inside. A few minutes later, she came walking around the side of the house carrying a little white cardboard box. Bud whispered to Peggy, "Uh-oh. Here she goes." It was the same old trick she had pulled on every child in Whistle Stop.

Idgie winked at them, and then said to her niece, "Hey, Ruthie, look what I just found out in the backyard. Do you want to see?"

Ruthie was curious and ran right over. "What is it?" She stood very still and watched with anticipation as Idgie slowly lifted the lid off the box. Inside the box, lying on a piece of cotton, was a human finger. Idgie said, "Look, Ruthie, somebody lost a finger."

Ruthie's eyes widened as she stared at the finger in the box. Then Idgie said, "Oh, look, Ruthie . . . it's moving."

Then Ruthie squealed, "Oh, Aunt Idgie. That's *your* finger in there!"

Idgie laughed and looked over at Bud and Peggy. "She's too smart for me. I can see, I'm gonna have to get up pretty early in the morning to fool you, Ruthie Threadgoode."

The next day they were in Florida, they all went fishing and swimming and ate lots of seafood, and Bud, Peggy, and Ruthie all got sunburned.

Every day afterward, Idgie would take Ruthie to work with her at the fruit stand and introduce her to everybody who stopped by. "This is my niece, Ruthie. She's so smart, she might be the next president of the United States, or a movie star. We haven't decided yet, have we, Ruthie?"

A few days later, Idgie said to Peggy and Bud, "Hey, you two, I have a question. Could I borrow Ruthie for a couple of days? I promise to take real good care of her."

Peggy said, "Sure, that's fine with us."

That night after dinner, Idgie came out on the porch and said, "Hey, Miss Ruthie, would you like to take a little trip with me tomorrow?"

"Where're we going?"

"It's a surprise, but I'll give you a hint. Close your eyes and don't look until I tell you to." When Ruthie opened her eyes, Idgie had on a Mickey Mouse hat with big round mouse ears. "Guess where we're going."

"Where?"

"Disney World! I know a few of the people who work there,

and we have two all-day passes to do anything we want. But we'd have to get up pretty early tomorrow. So, do you want to go?"

Ruthie started jumping up and down. "Yes! Yes!" She looked over at Peggy. "Momma, can I go? Please, please?"

At six-thirty the next morning, Idgie and Ruthie were on the road to Orlando to spend two days at Walt Disney World. A friend of Idgie's was the manager of one of the hotels there, and as a surprise, had booked an entire suite for them. As soon as they checked in and unpacked, they ran out, jumped on the tram, shot over to the park, and hit the ground running. For two days straight they ate all the junk food they could handle. Popcorn, ice cream, candy, hot dogs on a stick, you name it they ate it. They rode all the rides, and rode Dumbo the Flying Elephant and Peter Pan's Flight twice. Ruthie had her photo taken with Snow White, Goofy, and Cinderella, and both nights they went to the big fireworks display and drank hot chocolate.

On the second day, after they had ridden in the giant tea cups, they were walking down Main Street U.S.A., when Idgie saw Mickey Mouse himself standing on the corner waving at people. She immediately grabbed Ruthie by the hand and headed over. "Hey there, Mickey. I'm Idgie and this is my niece, Ruthie, from Maryland. I sure would love to get a picture of you two." Mickey answered in his little high-pitched Mickey Mouse voice, "Certainly, I'd be happy to." While they were posing, Idgie said, "We sure love your place, Mickey. I'm guessin' this is about the happiest place in the world." Mickey did a little dance and said, "Thank you, Idgie, we think so." Then they headed over to the Country Bear Jamboree.

ON THE THIRD day, when they arrived back home, Idgie's car was full of stuffed toys, Mickey Mouse balloons, two Donald Duck hats, a music box that played "It's a Small World," and a white plastic Snow White purse.

As they were helping to unload the car, Peggy said to Bud, "Look at all that stuff she bought her. She is going to spoil her rotten."

Bud smiled. "Oh, let her. She's only a kid once, and honestly I don't know who is having more fun, Ruthie or Aunt Idgie."

The next afternoon, Peggy and Bud were watching Ruthie, who was sitting out in the front yard talking with Idgie. Several of the neighborhood children had come over and were hanging on Idgie's every word, as she told them one tall tale after another.

Bud said, "Look at her, Peggy. After all these years, she's still the pied piper, isn't she?"

THE MORNING THEY were leaving to go back to Maryland, Idgie walked them out to the car. Ruthie had her arm around Idgie's waist and looked sad.

Idgie gave her a little squeeze and said, "Ruthie, now, what did I tell you?"

"That I'm the prettiest, the smartest, and the bravest girl in the world."

"What else?"

"Brave girls don't cry."

"That's right. And if these two ever give you any trouble, you call me and Aunt Idgie'll come up and give them a good whooping, you hear?"

Ruthie smiled a little and nodded and climbed into the back seat. Idgie turned to Bud and Peggy. "Thanks for coming to see me. I'm telling you, that little girl is gonna set the world on fire someday, you just wait and see. I just wish Ruth had lived long enough to meet her."

"Me, too," said Bud.

Idgie peered into the back seat. "Bye-bye, Ruthie. You come back and see me soon, y'hear?"

As they pulled away, Ruthie watched Idgie wave until she was out of sight, and then she started to cry.

"What's the matter, honey?"

"I don't want to leave Aunt Idgie."

Peggy said, "I know, sweetheart, but we'll be back."

THEY MEANT TO come back. But Bud and Peggy got busy with the clinic, and time got away from them. And on every birthday, Ruthie couldn't wait for the big wooden box with four jars of honey and two dozen big oranges that would come from Florida with the note

For Miss Ruthie
Bee happy
Love, Aunt Idgie

But a few years later, Ruthie removed the photo of herself and Mickey Mouse that she had stuck on her vanity mirror, and replaced it with a picture of her current boy crush. And soon that magical two-week visit to Florida became just a vague memory of a happy time.

Ruthie and Brooks

MITZI GRAHAM, a cute, plump young woman in a khaki skirt, was sitting downstairs with her legs draped over the arm of a chair, smoking a Kent cigarette and complaining to her sorority sisters about her new roommate. "It's just my luck to get Ruthie Threadgoode, the prettiest girl on campus, for a roommate. And it's not fair. I swear, if I had her legs and my boobs, I could rule the world."

She took another puff. "And then there are those ridiculously long eyelashes of hers and that skin to die for. Honestly, I have to spend at least a half hour getting made up and fixing my hair before I can show my face, and she just jumps up out of bed, brushes her teeth, throws on any old thing, and heads on out the door looking like she stepped out of a fashion magazine." Another puff. "And the worst part is, as much as I want to hate her, she's so damn nice, I can't even do that. I don't think she even knows how good-looking she is. When we're walking to class I see all the boys staring at her, and she never seems to notice."

It was true. Over the years, Ruthie Threadgoode had grown into quite a beauty. She had always received a lot of male attention, but by her sophomore year of college, she had begun to turn down more dates than she accepted. The boys were either too aggressive, too dull, or too something that did not appeal to her. She realized it was going to be hard and maybe even impossible for her to find someone who would be as interesting and as fun as her daddy. And so far, the boys she had been even slightly interested in had not met her standards for the kind of man she would want as a husband. So she'd made up her mind to stop wasting her time and concentrate on pursuing a career. She was interested in interior design and had landed a summer job working at *Southern Living* magazine, and this coming year had another one lined up at *Better Homes and Gardens*. But all those plans were made before she met Brooks Lee Caldwell.

ONE SATURDAY MORNING, Ruthie had her towel and soap and was walking down the hall to the bathroom to take her shower. Mitzi was trailing close behind, pleading with her. "You just *have* to go, Ruthie. For my sake. Please? My brother said if you would go out with Brooks, he would fix me up with Tubbs Newsome. They're frat brothers."

Ruthie made a little face. "Oh, honey, you know the boys at that house are not really my cup of tea."

"Why not? It's the best house on campus."

"Oh, I don't know, they just seem a little stuck-up and full of themselves to me."

Mitzi followed her into the bathroom. "Some of them are, but not Brooks. My mother knows his mother. He's real sweet. Just one little date? Please, Ruthie. I think Tubbs is the cutest thing. If I miss my one chance to go out with him, I just might eat six dozen donuts and kill myself. Then you'll be sorry."

Ruthie laughed. "Well, all right then, one date. Just for you."

"Oh, Ruthie, thank you, thank you, thank you," Mitzi said.

"You're welcome. Now may I take my shower?"

. . .

Brooks Lee Caldwell, a junior majoring in business admin-
istration, had seen Ruthie only once. She'd been sprinting across
campus, late for a class. As she ran by, Brooks punched his friend.
"Who is *that*?"

"That's Ruthie Threadgoode."

"You know her?"

"Yeah, I've met her. She's my sister's roommate. She's from
Maryland, I think. Why?"

"Why? I think I'm in love, that's why. Can you get me a date?"

"Oh, I might, if you could see fit to loan me your car next
weekend. Me and Alice are going to sneak off to her folks' apartment in Washington."

"Listen," Brooks said, "if you can get me a date with her, I'll
give you the car for a month. How come I never saw her before?"

"Because you always have your nose in some economics book.
See what you've been missing?"

The following weekend, Ruthie and Brooks had a double date
with Mitzi and Tubbs. When Brooks arrived to pick her up that
night, he was pretty much what Ruthie had expected. He had the
same look that all the preppy guys on campus had: slicked-back
straight hair, clean white button-down shirt, loafers with no socks.
He was definitely not her type, but there was no denying that he
was good-looking.

All through dinner, for Mitzi's sake, Ruthie had tried to be
most attentive and charming, but Brooks saw her glance down at
her watch a few times. At the end of the evening, when Brooks
walked her up to the door, he said, "Listen, Ruthie, I know this
was a blackmail date, and I probably won't ever see you again. But
may I at least hug you goodbye?"

Ruthie was a little thrown by the request. A hug was not the usual thing boys wanted at the end of the evening, but his arms were already around her, and before she knew it she felt herself melt into his body. And to her surprise, she couldn't tell where she ended and he began. It was a perfect fit. Like finding the right piece of the puzzle. His hug was not too rough or too weak. It was just right. She suddenly felt like Goldilocks. And he smelled so good, too.

After he let go and said good night and began walking back to his car, Ruthie heard herself say, "Um, Brooks?"

"Yes?" he said.

"Ah . . . could we do this again, sometime?"

Brooks looked at her and, with a sigh of sheer relief, wiped his brow and said, "Whew . . . Thank God. I was walking as slowly as I could. Tomorrow night?"

She nodded.

He cocked his head. "Promise me you won't get married before then?"

"I promise."

Ruthie watched as Brooks ran to his car. When he got there, he turned around and waved at her and then bowed from the waist. At that moment, Ruthie thought to herself, "Oh no. The boy has a sense of humor to match his good looks." She knew then she was either in terrible trouble, or on the verge of something wonderful.

Dot Weems

FAIRHOPE, ALABAMA

1985

Special Newsflash: Peggy Threadgoode just called to tell us that their daughter Ruthie is almost twenty-one years old and is now engaged to an Atlanta boy, Mr. Brooks Lee Caldwell, and they will be married in the spring. Congratulations to all! How do the names "Grandmother" and "Granddaddy" sound? Get ready, it will happen before you know it.

Speaking of that, is it just me, or are all of you taking more pills than you used to? This morning I looked at all the bottles of pills that Wilbur and I are taking every day: high blood pressure, heart pills, blood thinners, diuretics, calcium, fiber, cholesterol pills, laxative pills, you name it, we take it.

I hate to admit it, but I guess I must be getting old. Did you know that squirrels can remember where they've hidden over 10,000 nuts, and half the time I can't find my one pair of reading glasses. Never thought a squirrel was smarter than I am, but a fact is a fact, folks!

Your faithful scribe,

Dot

P.S. Just read where they think there might be life on Mars. I find it amusing that people are so curious about life on other planets, when so many don't even know their own neighbors!

Different Backgrounds

RUTHIE THREADGOODE HAD waited so long to turn twenty-one. She had dreamed about this day for years. She had visualized herself as being calm, cool, sure of herself, a woman of the world. But when her twenty-first birthday finally arrived, she was feeling a little bit insecure.

The year before, she had fallen in love with the most wonderful boy, Brooks Lee Caldwell. They were now engaged, and this should have been the happiest time in her life.

Ruthie knew she loved Brooks, but after meeting his family, it was painfully obvious that they came from very different backgrounds. Her family was not poor, by any means. Her father made a good living. But the Threadgoodes were definitely not "old money" like Brooks's family. The Lees and the Caldwells were two of the top old-monied families in Atlanta. Their house was located behind large black wrought iron gates and was a showcase. It had been regularly featured in *The Great Homes of Atlanta* magazine.

After spending the first weekend at their home at Number One Caldwell Circle, Ruthie felt that Brooks's father seemed to like her. But his mother, Martha Lee, was a different story. Although Martha Lee had never been anything but polite to her while she was there, Ruthie had felt an aloofness and sensed an ever-so-slight aura of disapproval.

No matter how many times she visited, Ruthie was still afraid she might do something wrong, spill something on one of their beautiful oriental rugs, or knock something over and break it. Or pick up the wrong fork at dinner.

Doubly hard was when Ruthie learned that after they were married, she and Brooks would be moving into the large and lovely home at Two Caldwell Circle, right next door to her in-laws. Ruthie had expressed her concern to Brooks and told him she thought it might be better if their first home together could be something a little smaller and maybe not so close to his parents. But Brooks didn't really understand the problem and explained that he couldn't turn down the house without hurting his parents' feelings. She loved him so much, what could she do? But it was going to be hard, taking care of such a large house, and living so close to someone who made her feel nervous. And, harder still, considering she loved animals and had been around them all her life, was that there were to be absolutely no dogs or cats allowed anywhere on Caldwell Circle. Martha Lee was deathly allergic to animal hair.

In fact, Martha Lee was not really allergic to animal hair, but saying so had ended the discussion. A little white lie was permissible when so much was at stake. She had worked too hard collecting her beautiful objets d'art over the years to take a chance. She had many expensive antique tapestries hanging on the walls, and she certainly didn't want some cat scratching at them or some dog running rampant through the house knocking over any of her priceless Chinese vases. She had one of the most exquisite homes in Atlanta, and she was going to keep it that way.

Martha Lee Caldwell was not a particularly tall lady, but her perfect posture made her seem so. Though she wasn't naturally beautiful, her high cheekbones and shiny black hair, which she wore slicked back in a tight, fashionable chignon, gave her a stunning and imposing appearance.

She also had a certain air about her that so many people envy and so few have. Her secret? Martha Lee was extremely pleased to be Martha Lee.

Being human, she'd naturally had her share of disappointments, but she'd been able to rise above any adversity. No matter what life threw at her, she could always cheer herself by reminding herself that thanks to her Philadelphia great-grandmother on her father's side, she was a direct descendant of the beautiful Duchess Carolyn Lee, wife of Duke Edmond James Lee, owner of the stately Lee Manor in Yorkshire, England, a fact she would often let drop into the most casual of conversations, even with perfect strangers. A large portrait of Duchess Carolyn Lee hung over the fireplace in her living room and was seen by anyone who entered. True, it was only a commissioned reproduction of an original portrait. But no matter. After all, she was family.

At Caldwell Circle

ATLANTA, GEORGIA

WHEN MARTHA LEE Caldwell first heard Brooks was engaged, she had been caught completely off guard. Brooks had called sounding thrilled that the Maryland girl had just agreed to marry him, and Martha Lee couldn't believe it. Dating the girl was one thing, but engaged to be married? She demanded that he come home immediately so they could discuss it.

After Brooks had talked to his father in private and had assured him the girl was not pregnant, his mother cornered him in the library and began peppering him with questions. Poor Brooks was trying as hard as he could to point out Ruthie's many wonderful qualities but was having no luck.

"She may be in a top sorority, but so are a lot of girls," Martha Lee said.

"But, Mother, she's not just in it, she's the president. And she was voted homecoming queen. Ruthie's one of the most popular girls on campus. She's really a terrific girl. The truth is, Mother, I'm lucky she's marrying me. She's had a lot of guys after her."

"That's all very well and good, but we really don't know who her people are, or where they're from."

"I told you."

"I know you told me, but really, Brooks, think about it. If you had said Mobile, Montgomery, or even Birmingham, I might be able to hold my head up. But Whistle Stop, Alabama? And I shudder to think where they came from before they landed there."

"Mother, please don't be so snooty. Besides, her family hasn't lived in Whistle Stop for years. I don't think Ruthie has ever even been there. And her father is a well-known doctor in Maryland."

"Oh, Brooks, he's not a real doctor. He's a *veterinarian,* for God's sake. His patients are dogs and cats—what do they know? My point is, you are my only son. I am only thinking about your future and what is best for you." She made a sad face. "Oh, Brooksie, aren't there some nice Atlanta girls you like? God knows, I'm not name proud, but Threadgoode? It sounds like an ad for a seamstress."

"Mother . . ."

"All right. I'm not ashamed to admit it. The Caldwell and the Lee families come from a long line of good stock, and we have an obligation to adhere to certain guidelines."

Brooks rolled his eyes.

"I didn't make this up, Brooks. It's a law of nature. Her father, the vet that you're so crazy about, would agree with me. You don't mate a thoroughbred racehorse with a Shetland pony."

"Oh, for God's sake, Mother, you're living in another century. Nobody cares about those things anymore. You'll just have to meet them and see for yourself."

Martha Lee could see she was not making progress. The boy was smitten and insisted that they meet the girl's parents.

A FEW WEEKS later, after having met Bud and Peggy Threadgoode, who had driven down from Maryland to Atlanta for the occasion, Martha Lee was talking with her husband at the dinner table.

"Linwood, you have got to talk to Brooks about marrying that girl, before it's too late."

"What do you mean?"

"Just what I said. Now, the parents seem perfectly nice, but—"

"No more buts about it, Martha. The boy has made up his mind and he won't back down. Nor should he. As far as I can tell the girl is terrific."

"I'll tell you what she is. A veterinarian's daughter whose family is from some little Podunk hole-in-the-wall hick Alabama town that nobody's ever heard of."

Linwood closed his eyes and sighed. "Martha, no matter what your or my reservations may be, he is going to marry the girl. And it's time for us to make every effort to welcome her and her parents into the family."

"But Linwood . . ."

He put his hand up. "Let me finish, Martha. Like it or not, you're going to have to accept the fact that one day, the Threadgoodes will be grandparents to our grandchildren. I don't know why you're so upset. I thought they were perfectly respectable. He struck me as being a rather delightful guy, very personable, and the wife seemed very nice."

Martha Lee sat there and pouted for a moment. Then she put down her fork and pulled out the last arrow in her quiver. "All right, Linwood, I didn't want to have to tell you this. . . . I had Gerta do a little research on the good doctor and his wife, the ones you insist are so perfectly respectable."

Linwood put down his fork. "Oh no . . . Martha, you didn't."

"Yes, I did. Were you aware that his mother ran some kind of a railroad cafe, slinging hash for a living? And according to Gerta, his father was some man from Georgia named Frank Bennett, who evidently just disappeared completely out of the picture before he was even born. Left the mother flat. Mind you, that's only *his* side of the family. Who knows about the mother's side. Her folks probably worked for the railroad laying track or something."

"So they worked for a living. So what?"

"So what? How are we supposed to socialize with these people? We have absolutely nothing in common." Then she made a face. "And the father has that funny arm. And I certainly can't take the mother to the club."

"Why? She seemed very nice."

"*Why?* Oh for God's sake, Linwood. The woman wears polyester pants, and collects frog figurines."

"What?"

You heard me, *frogs!* The woman has over two hundred frogs. And she told me she had just found the cutest one dressed up as Batman. Need I say more?" Martha Lee heaved a deep sigh and said, "When I think that Brooks could have married into the Coca-Cola family or the Georgia-Pacific lumber family. But no, he picks some little nobody, from a nobody family from a nowhere place." Then, totally out of character, Martha Lee burst into tears and began sobbing into her white linen monogrammed table napkin.

Her husband went over and put his arms around her. "Oh, Martha, it will be all right. You'll see."

She looked up at him tearfully and nodded. "It's just that I'm so terribly disappointed."

AFTER THEIR FIRST meeting with the Caldwells at their home, all Bud had said to his daughter was, "Honey, you know your mother and I think the world of Brooks, and we couldn't be happier that you're marrying him, but just be aware that you're landing in some pretty high cotton."

"I know," said Ruthie.

"Do you think you're up for that?"

"I think so, Daddy."

"Okay then, you know you have our full blessing. I'll get myself all prettied up, and I promise I will be the best lookin' father of the bride they've ever seen."

Six months later, at the wedding, Martha Lee had some small consolation. At least she could introduce the father of the bride as Dr. Threadgoode. She just prayed no one would ask what kind of a doctor. And as for the mother, she was sweet. But they were never going to be best friends.

Dot Weems

Just a short update: I'm sure you have all heard about my mishap by now. Nobody's fault but my own. I was so busy looking down at my grocery list, and I wasn't paying attention to where I was going. But I am okay now. And I have a new hip that is working fine.

Under the heading "You're Never Too Old to Learn": I thought I had known this before, but I never really realized just how much we all depend on other human beings, until I got hit by a truck in the Walmart parking lot and had my leg cut open. The minute it happened, total strangers came running from all over and gathered around me. One lady immediately called an ambulance; another sat down beside me and held my hand. A man ran and pulled a blanket out of his camper and covered me up so I wouldn't go into shock. And they all, to a person, stayed right there with me, until the ambulance came.

They said later that if it hadn't been for everybody's fast action—from the people in the parking lot, to the ambulance drivers, and the ER doctors and nurses—I could have bled to death. People I'd never met before in my life, who didn't know me from Adam's cat, suddenly became the most important people in the world. All helped save my life, and I don't even know their names. Except for the poor guy who hit me, bless his heart. It wasn't even his fault. But he came to the hospital every day just to make sure I was okay.

My point is: From now on, no matter how hard the doom-and-gloomers try, they'll never convince me the world is a terrible place and people are just no good. I know there are some rotten apples out there, but take it from me, this old world of ours, flawed as it may be, is a much better place than you have been told.

By the way, I read a quote from William A. Ward and thought I would pass it on. "God gave you 86,400 seconds a day. Have you used one to say 'Thank you'?"

I sure did when I lived to tell the tale!

The other good news is that I received a call from Bud and Peggy Threadgoode telling me that their daughter, Ruthie, just gave birth to their first grandchild, a girl, named Carolyn Lee. Oh my, isn't it amazing how fast time flies. It seems like just yesterday when Ruthie was born. How old am I? On that subject, don't ask, and I won't tell.

Anyhow, congrats to mother and child.

Love to all,
Dot

P.S. Idgie sent me a funny joke I'll pass along: Put out with your relatives? Just remember, even the best family tree has its sap.

Silver Spring, Maryland

1989

On Sunday morning, Bud was outside in the garage at his work table, busy repairing a birdhouse, when he heard Peggy calling out in a loud voice: "Oh my God. Oh my God. Bud, get in here quick!"

Bud immediately grabbed a hammer, then ran inside the house, ready to defend her from who knows what. "Where are you?" he yelled.

"In here!"

"In here" was at the kitchen table. Peggy was sitting by the window looking at herself in a round mirror about the size of a pancake.

Bud said, "What's wrong? Are you all right?

She looked up at him accusingly. "Why didn't you tell me I have a wattle?"

"A what?"

"A wattle! Look at my neck! I have a wattle under my chin. Right here . . . see?"

He walked over and looked.

"Do you see that?" she said, moving some skin under her chin back and forth. "I have a definite wattle!"

He looked closer and was baffled. "I don't see anything, honey, maybe a little loose skin."

"Bud, it's not just loose skin. It's a wattle! I know a wattle when I see one, and I have a wattle."

He could tell she had made up her mind, and he was in a no-win situation. If he agreed she had a wattle, she would be upset. If he didn't, she would still be upset. She continued staring at herself in the mirror. "I can't believe you never noticed it. Look," she said, turning her head back and forth. "Oh, I'm *not* aging well."

"Honey, you look just fine to me. I don't notice anything different. You still look like your beautiful self to me."

"That's because you're my husband, and you're looking at me through the eyes of love. But trust me. Other people notice."

Bud could see that Peggy was really upset, and he tried his best to figure out some way to make her feel better. He finally said, "Hey, Red, how about I take you out to the Country Corner for lunch? A little fried okra? Black-eyed peas? Some good ole cornbread? That might cheer you up. What d'ya say?"

"Oh sure, Bud. And have everyone there say, 'Oh look, there's Doctor Threadgoode having lunch with his mother.'"

He laughed and went over and hugged her. "Oh, honey, come on," he said. "It's not that serious. Get dressed, and after lunch I'll take you out to the shopping mall. How 'bout it?"

Peggy did love the cornbread at the Country Corner and the shopping mall, and after a long moment she gave in.

"Well, all right. But promise me one thing."

"What?"

"Promise me you won't ever get glasses."

"I promise. You will always be just a beautiful blur."

Peggy hated getting older. But Bud didn't care. He loved the way she looked, even her freckles that she hated. She'd look at herself and say, "I look just like Howdy Doody."

As Bud said later, "Women look in the mirror and think they look terrible. Men never look and think they look great. And most times both are wrong."

Callaway Resort and Gardens

DOT WEEMS WAS right about time flying by. Ruthie's seven-year-old daughter, Carolyn Lee, now had a four-year-old little brother named Richard.

This Thanksgiving, Brooks and Ruthie had decided to take them to the Callaway Gardens resort in Pine Mountain, Georgia, for the week, and had rented one of the large cabins by the lake. Bud and Peggy had driven down from Maryland to spend Thanksgiving with them and had just left to go back home.

Brooks and Ruthie were down at the lake watching the kids playing with a few other children. Brooks said, "You were right. I guess I needed a break more than I realized. Of course, Mother is still having a fit we didn't spend Thanksgiving with her at the club. But it was so good to see your mom and dad."

Ruthie called out, "Carolyn, stop hitting your brother, and give him his hat back. . . . Now, please." Then she turned to Brooks and said, "It was good to see them. I know it was hard to say no to your mother, but I want the kids to know their other grandparents. They see your mother every day."

"You're right."

Brooks sat back in his chair, kicked off his shoes, and put his feet in the sand. "You know, Ruthie, I sure do admire your dad.

He told me that he'd always wanted to be a veterinarian, from the time he was a kid, and he didn't let anything stop him."

"That's Daddy. He always said you could be anything you wanted, if you tried hard enough."

Brooks looked a little wistful and said, "When I was growing up, I wanted to be—now don't laugh—a forest ranger."

"Really? You never told me that."

"Yeah. I used to spend hours in the woods behind the house. I always wanted to live in a log cabin by a lake, away from the rat race . . . but that's not going to happen."

"Why not? If that's what you wanted to do, I'd be happy."

Brooks looked at her and smiled. "You would, too, wouldn't you? God, I don't know how I got so lucky to get you. You're the best."

"Thank you, but, sweetheart, I mean it. I don't need a big house or anything. I want you to do something you love."

"I know you do. But it was just a kid's dream. Besides, Dad's counting on me to step in and take over the business. When he was my age, he did the same for Granddaddy. And he's the last person on earth I would want to let down. He depends on me. I promised him if anything ever happened to him I'd keep the business going and take care of Mother. And I know it's hard, and you're a good sport to hang in there with her. But it won't be forever, I promise." Brooks paused for a moment. "Here's something I've been thinking about lately. Ruthie, after the kids grow up, let's you and me just up and sell the house, and buy ourselves a small place in the mountains somewhere and then take off and travel. I'd love to take you to Paris, and London, and Rome. Maybe buy a big motor home and then just drive around the country, seeing things."

Ruthie was surprised. "A motor home? Can you imagine the look on your mother's face if we bought a motor home?"

Brooks laughed. "No, frankly, I can't. But how about it?"

"Sweetheart, if that's what you want, we'll do it. Just promise me you'll stop working so hard. The kids and I hardly ever see you anymore."

"I will, but this is just a particularly tough time right now. When Dad got sick, he left a lot of things that have to be taken care of, and, unfortunately, I'm the only one who can do it."

Just then Carolyn screamed from the edge of the lake. "Mother! Make Richard stop splashing me!"

Richard yelled, "She splashed me first!"

"I did not."

"Did, too."

Ruthie looked over at Brooks as the two kids continued to splash and scream at each other. "Remind me. Whose idea was it to have children?"

Brooks laughed. "I can't remember now."

Bud in a Nutshell

SILVER SPRING, MARYLAND
2009

ALTHOUGH HIS HAIR was now completely silver, Bud Thread-goode was still a tall, good-looking man. This morning he was sitting at his desk talking to his daughter on the phone, as he did every Sunday. And after he hung up, he had to smile. Sometimes Ruthie just tickled him to death. She was always coming up with the craziest things she wanted him to do. Get his hair styled, buy new glasses, get a brand-new prosthetic arm with all the bells and whistles, quit wearing his old worn-out wool plaid jacket from the fifties, take up golf. Never anything he wanted to do; however, after protesting as hard as he could, in the end, he always wound up doing what she wanted. Well, almost everything. He still wore his favorite old plaid jacket when she wasn't around.

Later that afternoon, when Peggy was sleeping, Bud figured he might as well get this one over with, so he sat down at his desk, pulled out a piece of plain white paper, and picked up his pen.

For Ruthie, Carolyn, and Richard, and anyone else who might give a hoot about an old Alabama coot.

I begin my life history, memoir, or whatever you may deem to call it, by confessing it is only being written be-cause my daughter wants me to. I have no illusions of my

life being so important that it needs to be set down on
paper. However, Ruthie read an article saying that everyone
should write out a life history for their family to have in the
future. And they should do it while they still remember it.
So here goes.

Me in a Nutshell: A Brief History

My name is James Buddy Threadgoode, Jr., at present seventy-nine years of age. I was born at home on December 14, 1929, in the small railroad town of Whistle Stop, Alabama. Upon my arrival into the world, everybody told me that I was the cutest baby they had ever seen, however, since then I have heard that very same sentiment expressed concerning other babies, including some not so cute.

My mother was Ruth Anne Jamison, born in Valdosta, Georgia, in the year 1905. My father was Frank Corley Bennett, also of Valdosta. At the time of my birth, my parents were separated and my mother was living with friends in Alabama.

Although I never knew my father, I have no complaints. I was legally adopted by the Threadgoode family and named for their son Buddy, who died before I was born. I can honestly say I had a very happy childhood. I was raised mostly by two women, my mother and her best friend, Idgie Threadgoode, with a lot of help from the entire town. I was really no different from most other children in Whistle Stop. I did lose half my arm in a stupid railroad accident when I was six, but as far as I can recall, I was happy most of the time, and was certainly the most well-fed kid in town. My mother and my Aunt Idgie owned and ran the town's cafe. When you live in the back of a cafe, you can bet you never go hungry.

Sadly, I lost my mother to cancer in 1947. After graduating

from high school, due to some strong encouragement from my Aunt Idgie—in the form of a threat to kick me in the behind if I didn't—I attended college at Georgia Tech, then transferred to Auburn University to study veterinary medicine. In 1954, I married the prettiest girl in Alabama, by the name of Peggy Ann Hadley, and never regretted it. I have had a sweetheart all my life. In the year 1966, after my stint in the U.S. Army, we moved to Silver Spring, Maryland. In 1964, my wife and I were blessed with our daughter, Ruthie, who has given me the grandest gift in the world, two grandchildren to spoil.

Ruthie says to be sure and sprinkle in some history, and so I will add that when I was a child, the president was Franklin Delano Roosevelt, and I remember listening to him over the radio. One of the great joys of my childhood was listening to the radio and going to the picture show once a week. I was raised during the Great Depression, although it did not affect me in any way that I can remember. Aunt Idgie grew her own vegetables in the lot in back of the cafe, and we always kept plenty of chickens and hogs. I would say the greatest day in history that I personally lived through was VJ Day, 1945. When the news came over the radio, everybody in Whistle Stop went running out into the streets yelling, and banging on pots and pans. And on every train that came through town that day, there were people hanging out of the windows, yelling at the top of their lungs, so happy the war was over and our boys were coming home. The second-best day was probably in July of 1969, seeing our guys land on the moon.

I've made some money in my time, but all my life, I've had something that no amount of money could buy. I've had people who loved me and who I loved right back.

I think that's about it, unless something noteworthy happens to me in the next few years I have left, which I sincerely doubt, since at seventy-nine, I'm pretty much over the hill.

And so in closing, as the kids say, I am sending a great big shout-out to all the great-grandkids yet to come down the line. It's too bad you never got to meet me, because I have often been told that I am the cutest old man they ever met and a hell of a lot of fun. So goodbye for now, and here's wishing you all the good luck you can handle.

S.O.B. *(aka Sweet Ol' Bud)*

BUD HAD RETIRED from the army a full captain, and he used to joke that he was a vet who was a vet. When he'd first expressed his desire to become a veterinarian, a lot of people had their doubts, but not Peggy, and certainly not his Aunt Idgie. As usual, she had been behind him 100 percent. She'd just said, "You can do it."

But Bud wasn't a fool. He knew being a doctor with one arm was not going to be a stroll in the park. Still, it was nothing compared to what others had to deal with. He'd seen it firsthand. In 1945, right after the war, boys had come home with half their faces blown off, or with both arms and legs missing. Some came back suffering from such severe shell shock, they couldn't stop shaking.

So, as far as he was concerned, missing an arm was sometimes "a pain in the ass" and inconvenient at best. But at least it hadn't been his right arm, and it was pretty amazing what he could do with one good right arm and his new top-of-the-line artificial arm. When people asked Peggy how he did it, she would say it helped that he had a great sense of humor. Although he was very serious about his work, one of his most charming traits was that he never took himself very seriously. As he often said, "Half an arm is better than half a brain."

Although Bud couldn't perform quite as well as other doctors physically, he excelled at diagnostics and treatment options. Consequently, after he left the army he was offered his own clinic in Silver Spring, Maryland. At first, he and Peggy weren't happy about being so far away from Idgie, but it was a great opportunity. When he called and asked her what she thought, Idgie'd said, "Good for you, Buddy. Sounds like a great deal." When he had expressed concern about living so far away from her, she just said, "Don't you worry about me. I'll always be right here. And who knows, one day I just might show up there and surprise you." That was Aunt Idgie, all right. She had always been full of surprises.

The Bee Charmer

As usual, as soon as it was spring, six-year-old Buddy Thread-goode, Jr., was running around town barefooted, and this time he stepped on a nail and couldn't get it out. When he hobbled into the cafe and showed it to his mother and Idgie, Idgie immediately picked him up, threw him over her shoulder, and walked him over to Dr. Hadley's house. After the doctor had removed the nail, cleaned the wound, and bandaged his foot, Idgie took him home and put him in the back room. Buddy sat in bed with his foot up and read comic books for the rest of the morning, which was okay with him.

Idgie ran back inside the cafe just in time to help with the last of the breakfast rush, and an anxious Ruth wanted to know how Buddy was. Idgie grinned and grabbed an apron. "Just fine. He didn't even cry. Didn't make a peep. Doc Hadley said he'd never seen such a brave boy."

"Really?"

"Yep. He was fine, but I almost fainted when Doc was pulling that nail out. But Buddy did great. I would have yelled my head off."

Idgie was so proud of Buddy for being so brave that she decided she wanted to do something extra special for him as a reward. Later that afternoon, after the lunch dishes were done, Idgie went to the back room, picked up Buddy's jacket and hat, and said, "Hey, little man, put these on. We're going somewhere."

"Where?"

"Never you mind where. I have something I want to show you."

"What?"

"It wouldn't be a surprise if I told you, would it? But you have to promise me one thing. You won't tell your mother."

"I promise."

"Scout's honor?"

"Yes."

"Okay. Let's go."

Buddy jumped up. Wherever she was taking him, he knew it was going to be somewhere fun. They got in the car, and Idgie drove along the railroad tracks where he had never been.

"Where are we going?"

"You'll see soon enough, my boy." After a few minutes she turned onto a one-lane dirt road, and then stopped the car at the edge of a large green meadow out by Double Springs Lake and said, "This is it."

They got out and she led him over to a spot and said, "Buddy, sit down right here. And do not move. No matter what, don't move. Promise me, or I can't show you the surprise."

"I promise," he said. It was then that Buddy noticed she had something in her left jacket pocket.

"What's that?" he asked.

"Ahh . . . that's for me to know, and you to find out. You just stay right there and don't ask no more questions. You are about to see my secret magic trick." Buddy sat and watched as she walked over to a tree across the meadow. Idgie turned around and smiled at him, then pulled a glass jar out of her pocket and stuck her entire arm down inside a hole in the tree. Buddy could hardly believe what happened next. All of a sudden he heard a loud roar, and soon the tree and Idgie were covered with thousands of bees. He sat there with his mouth open as Idgie slowly pulled the jar—which was now full of honey—back out of the tree. She then turned and walked away with the bees still swarming all around her.

When she reached him, all Buddy could say was, "Whoa . . . whoa . . . how did you do that, Aunt Idgie?"

"I'm a natural-born bee charmer, that's how."

"You are? Wow, what's that?"

"Somebody that the bees like, that they don't sting."

Oh . . . wow. Does Momma know you're a bee charmer?"

Idgie made a face. "No! And you can't tell her, either, all right?"

"I won't."

"So now we have a special secret that nobody else in the whole word knows about. Just us."

"Wow," he said again.

Of course, that was a bald-faced lie. Ruth knew about the bee tree. Idgie had brought her to that very same tree years ago. But Idgie wanted Buddy to feel special today, because he was to her. And he always would be.

On their way home they stopped at his Aunt Ninny's house and gave her the jar of honey. She was most grateful. Ninny Threadgoode dearly loved biscuits and honey for breakfast. When they got back to the cafe late that afternoon, Ruth opened the door and smiled. "Where have you two rascals been?"

Idgie breezed right past her and said, "Oh, just out. Right, Buddy?"

"Yes ma'am, just out," said Buddy, trying not to laugh.

· · ·

LATER THAT NIGHT, after Buddy was in bed, Ruth looked at Idgie. "Well, Buddy sure seems in a good mood tonight. Where did you take him today?"

Idgie smiled and said, "I'll never tell. It's a secret."

Ruth laughed. "Oh, *you* and your secrets. I know you. I'll bet you drove him over to Gate City to that pool hall, didn't you?"

"My lips are sealed," Idgie said.

The fact that she had taken Buddy to the bee tree today was a pretty innocent little secret to keep from Ruth. But Idgie had another, not-so-innocent secret that she was keeping from her. She had to. She couldn't take a chance on losing Ruth and Buddy forever.

Atlanta, Georgia

AFTER SHE HAD received her father's life history, Ruthie felt a bit disappointed at how short it was, but not surprised. It was just like him to downplay all of his many accomplishments. He hadn't even mentioned the fact that he had once been a famous high school football star. She still had all the write-ups and headlines that had appeared in the Birmingham news. "ONE-ARMED QUARTERBACK LEADS WHISTLE STOP'S TEAM TO STATE CHAMPIONSHIP."

There were so many things he'd left out. He had also neglected to mention that he had started his own veterinary clinic and now had eight doctors and over twenty-something in staff working under him. Ruthie was his only child, but until the VFW gave him that big lifetime award even she hadn't known he'd volunteered so much time and money helping wounded veterans get back on their feet. Or that, in spite of his handicap, he had graduated second in his class at Auburn. And she wouldn't have known that if her mother hadn't told her. All her life, total strangers were always coming up to her, telling her about something nice her father had done for them. When she asked why he'd never told her any of these things, he would just smile and say, "Oh, honey, I guess I just forgot."

Her dad also had a habit of giving money away to every Tom, Dick, or Harry with a sob story, and not one animal brought to his clinic was ever refused treatment because of money. Her mother said it was a Threadgoode family trait. During the Depression, his Aunt Idgie had fed every poor person for miles around.

And as Ruthie's mother had pointed out, Bud was a terrible liar. One day her mother said to Ruthie, "Your father will tell a lie when the truth would have served him better. This morning I walked in the bathroom at the office and smelled cigarettes and I said, 'Bud, are you still smoking after you promised me to quit?' And he looked me right in the eye and said, 'I'm not smoking. That's catnip you're smelling.' And I said, 'Bud. I've smelled catnip before, and it doesn't smell like tobacco.' 'Oh,' he says. 'That's because it's a rare form of catnip that comes all the way from India.'"

Ruthie had to laugh. "Daddy sure can make up a tall tale, can't he?"

"Oh yes. He got that little trait from his Aunt Idgie. Now, you talk about tall tales. She could tell them all day long and with a straight face. One time, one of her hunting friends gave her this old ratty-looking stuffed deer head, so she promptly hung it up in the cafe and told everybody that it was the head of an extremely rare two-hundred-year-old Siberian antelope." Peggy laughed. "She used to pull all kinds of crazy stunts. My mother told me that one time Idgie snuck over to Reverend Scroggins's house on laundry day and stole his long underwear right off the line. She stuffed it with straw, put a hat on it, and stuck it on the front row of his church the next Sunday. She loved to play tricks.

"Oh yeah, Aunt Idgie was a real character, all right, and now that I think about it, way ahead of her time. She was an independent woman *long* before the women's movement came about. She ran her own business, and always did things her own way. I don't think she ever let anybody tell her what to do, except your grandmother Ruth. Now, Idgie'd listen to Ruth. I remember one time when Idgie got to drinking too much and hanging out down at that River Club playing poker in the back room till all hours. Now, I don't know what was said, but my mother told me that Ruth must have put her foot down pretty hard, because, after that, Idgie cleaned up her act in a hurry. I don't think she ever went back to that River Club again, either."

"What was Grandmother Ruth like?"

Peggy looked at her daughter and smiled.

"Oh . . . like you, really. You have her nice thick hair, only yours is a little lighter. She was more of a darker brunette. She was as tall as you are, slender and pretty. And so sweet. I went to the Bible class she taught at church and we all just adored her." Peggy sighed. "She died so young. Only forty-two. It was so sad. Everybody in Whistle Stop was at her funeral. Idgie and your poor daddy were just heartbroken. He went away to college pretty soon after that, and that was a help to get his mind off it. But you know, I don't think Aunt Idgie ever really got over it."

"How so?"

"Oh, after Ruth died, she kept the cafe open. She had promised her to make sure your daddy got through school. But after he graduated, she just shut the cafe down for good and took off for Florida."

"Did she ever go back?"

"No, I don't think she ever did, except maybe for a few funerals. Of course, Idgie being Idgie, when she moved to Florida, she made plenty of new friends. But I don't think she ever had another special friend . . . not like your grandmother was."

Losing Ninny

DOT WEEMS CALLED Idgie and Julian first and said she had just received news that their sister-in-law Ninny Threadgoode had passed away. The next morning, Julian and Idgie left for Alabama to make arrangements. It was a sad trip for both. Ninny had been married to their oldest brother, Cleo. Not only had Ninny been sweet, she'd always seen things a little differently from people. She seemed to see only the best in life and made friends everywhere she went.

Ninny was laid to rest with a small graveside service in the Threadgoode family plot, at the cemetery just behind what had been the old Whistle Stop Baptist Church. Besides Julian and Idgie, a few of the other old-timers were there. Opal Butts and Big George's wife, Onzell, and their daughter came over from Birmingham. Dot and Wilbur Weems drove up from Fairhope, and Grady Kilgore and his wife, Gladys, came from Tennessee. Reverend Scroggins's son, Jessie Ray, who was now preaching over in Birmingham, had conducted the service. It was so sad to see the old town and the church all shut down and boarded up. But thankfully, after the service a lady who had once been a neighbor of Ninny's had everybody over to her house in nearby Gate City for some food. After they had eaten, they all gathered on the front porch and talked about Ninny and the good old days, before the railroad yard closed down.

It was getting late in the day. Jessie Ray Scroggins and his wife left first, and as they drove away, Gladys Kilgore said to Idgie, "This is a hell of a way to spend Easter, isn't it? Having to say goodbye to sweet old Ninny."

Idgie didn't know that in April 1988, she would be making another sad trip to Whistle Stop, this time to bury her brother Julian. On that day, before she left to drive back home to Florida, she made one last stop back at the old cemetery and put something on Ruth's grave. It was an Easter card that she signed,

> *I'll always remember.*
> *Your friend,*
> *The Bee Charmer*

An Unexpected Turn of Events

BIRMINGHAM, ALABAMA

February 10, 2010

SOMEONE ONCE SAID, "It ain't over till the fat lady sings," and in Evelyn Couch's case, this was certainly true. She'd been well over forty, overweight, and depressed when her life had suddenly taken an unexpected turn. So unexpected, in fact, that not one person, particularly Evelyn, could have guessed how it would end.

Evelyn had been an accidental late-in-life baby, the only offspring of a cold mother and somewhat indifferent father. Their obvious lack of parental enthusiasm had made Evelyn feel as though she was always in the way.

From an early age she was shy and insecure. In high school, if there had been a category to vote for "Least Likely to Succeed," Evelyn would have won. She was so uncomfortable at being noticed that through four years of high school she had tiptoed through the halls with her head down; so afraid of making a mistake that when a teacher called on her, she would turn beet red and was often unable to speak.

And as the years went by, sadly nothing changed. When she and her husband had attended her fifteenth high school reunion, only a few of the girls remembered her, but not one of the boys did. Not surprising. She had never been the kind of girl boys asked out on a date. Having endured such a lack of male interest, Evelyn felt grateful to have a husband at all, even if he had been a hand-me-down. His first wife, a woman named Olive, had run away with her interior decorator.

Ed Couch, several years her senior, was working for her father at the local Firestone tire store. Her father had invited him home for dinner, and that was that.

Not that Ed wasn't perfectly nice, he was. And she loved him. However, the longer she was married to him, the more she understood the first wife. The truth was, Ed was not a romantic person. On their last wedding anniversary, he had given her a set of new bread knives and a toenail clipper. It was clear that something was missing in their relationship. Maybe if they had not had two children right away, it might have helped. Ed had not wanted children. He already had one son named Norris with his first wife, and he didn't like him very much.

After both of their children left home, Evelyn began to do everything she knew how to help their marriage. She had even enrolled in a "Put a Spark Back into Your Marriage" seminar, but as she found out later, you can't do that alone. The other party has to be willing. And after years of trying, she finally had to face facts. It wasn't that Ed didn't love her, he did. But he would rather watch football and eat. And soon, all they did together was eat. Sometimes she cooked, sometimes they went out to the cafeteria. It was some comfort.

But as the years went by, and she gained more and more weight, she found herself getting more and more depressed. She began to wonder what the point was of dragging herself through another dull, hopeless day just to face another one just like it.

Bored at home, she had gone with Ed to his weekly visit with his mother at the nursing home. She walked down to the visitors' lounge to wait for him, and she just happened to sit down next to an eighty-six-year-old lady from Whistle Stop, Alabama, named

Ninny Threadgoode. As Evelyn soon found out, Ninny just loved to talk. She told Evelyn the most wonderful stories about the two women who used to run the Whistle Stop Cafe and their little boy, Buddy.

Every week after that, when Ed was with his mother, Evelyn would sit and visit with Ninny, and before Evelyn knew it, she had made a friend. For some unknown reason, she wasn't shy with Ninny. And for the first time in Evelyn's life, someone saw things in her she couldn't see herself. Ninny didn't think she was too heavy at all, she thought she looked healthy. Ninny also thought she was pretty, and had a great smile and personality.

As the weeks went by and Evelyn confided in her friend about the depression she was going through and how hopeless she felt, Ninny encouraged her, and told her that she was far too young to give up on life. She advised Evelyn to start getting out in the world and meeting new people. Maybe get a job selling Mary Kay cosmetics.

With a little more confidence in herself and thanks to Ninny's encouragement, Evelyn took a chance and signed up for a Mary Kay starter kit. Six months later, against all odds, Evelyn Couch became one of Mary Kay's top saleswomen, and within the year was driving a brand-new pink Cadillac. Nobody was more surprised at her success than Evelyn. When she attended a Mary Kay convention in Dallas, Mary Kay herself pulled her aside and told her why she was doing so well. "Honey, people *like* you. You're not some high-powered intimidating salesperson, you're one of them. More like a sister, or a friend. They trust you, and they trust the product." Pretty soon after that, Ed started turning off the television set and paying more attention to her. As she was finding out, nothing succeeds like success!

. . .

WITH THE MONEY she'd made selling Mary Kay products, Evelyn Couch purchased a big new house over the mountain, a vacation home at the beach, and a brand-new RV that she and Ed drove to Mary Kay seminars all over the country. Mrs. Evelyn Couch, age 51, from Birmingham, Alabama, had become one of the company's most inspiring leaders. She and Ed traveled for years, and really had a lot of fun. Until they found out that Ed had diabetes. He would have to be put on dialysis, and could no longer travel. So she gave up her position with Mary Kay and stayed home with him. She missed the work and the traveling, but unbeknownst to her, another unexpected turn was just around the corner.

Over the years, Evelyn had been responsible for the sales of so many pink Cadillacs for her Mary Kay team that the owner of the big Cadillac dealership in Birmingham called and offered her a job.

Evelyn had worked on the showroom floor selling cars for only six months when the dealership's sales almost doubled. Her secret was having worked for Mary Kay for so many years. She knew how to sell to women. At the time, what most car salesmen didn't understand was that while it may have been the men who paid for the cars, it was usually the women who picked them out. They chose the model, the make, and the color. And thanks to the women's movement, more women were entering the workforce, and more women were buying their own cars. A year later, Evelyn had been made branch manager, and eventually she wound up buying the entire dealership.

"Couch Cadillac" had a nice ring to it, she thought.

In fact, she did her own television commercials. "Hi, this is Evelyn Couch, of Couch Cadillac, inviting you to come on in to one of my dealerships. Tell them Evelyn sent you, and I'll give you the deal of a lifetime on a brand-new Cadillac." Everyone said the ads were very effective. They must have been, because at her next high school class reunion, everybody there claimed to remember her, especially the men.

All this because twenty-five years earlier, she'd happened to sit down next to a kind lady named Ninny Threadgoode. Evelyn often wondered why she'd just happened to sit by her that day. Had it been fate? A chance meeting? A happy accident? Evelyn chose to believe it was fate. And it made her happy to think so.

And even now, so many years after her friend Ninny Threadgoode had passed away, Evelyn still kept a picture of her on her desk, and sometimes she even talked to it. And today was one of those days. After she hung up the phone, she looked at the photo of the sweet-looking old lady wearing a polka-dotted dress and said, "Ninny, you won't believe this, but some fool just called and offered me over a million dollars to buy Couch Cadillac, and I just might take it."

....

Atlanta, Georgia

BRIARWOOD MANOR
2013

WHEN HIS WIFE, Peggy, had been diagnosed with Alzheimer's disease, Bud decided to sell his veterinary practice so he could look after her. He took care of her at home for as long as he could until the doctor said that she needed to be placed in memory care with twenty-four-hour professional supervision. But as Bud and Ruthie quickly discovered, trying to find a good facility on such short notice was almost impossible.

But luckily for them, Martha Lee had very close ties with Briarwood Manor, a top-rated "continuing care" senior community right there in Atlanta with an excellent memory care unit onsite, and close to Ruthie. There was a three-year waiting list to get into Briarwood Manor, but it took Martha Lee only one phone call to get them admitted that day.

Getting them into Briarwood so quickly had not been an act of kindness on Martha Lee's part. She didn't want the Threadgoodes moving in next door with their daughter. Caldwell Circle was for immediate family only. Also, the thought that the mother might bring her ceramic frog collection terrified her.

After Bud and Peggy moved from Maryland to Briarwood Manor, Bud spent every day with her in the memory care unit, staying by her bedside, until she fell asleep at night. Even at the end, when she didn't know who he was anymore, he still came. She was still his Peggy and he could still hold her hand.

For those four years, Bud didn't give much thought to the future. After Peggy died, he found he was having a hard time adjusting to life without her. From the age of eighteen, he had been one-half of a couple, Bud and Peggy or Peggy and Bud. They had rarely been apart. She ran his office at the clinic, so they'd been together almost twenty-four hours a day. They had been so close it was almost as if they were the same person.

WHEN HER MOTHER died, Ruthie begged her daddy to leave Briarwood Manor and move in with her. However, he didn't think it was a very good idea.

"But, Daddy, I really want you here," she said.

"I know, honey, but I don't want to put anybody out or cause trouble. Martha Lee was so kind to get your mother and me in here. And if I just picked up and left, it might seem ungrateful. I'm fine right where I am."

But he really wasn't fine. He was a country boy at heart, and used to the outdoors and open spaces. Now he mostly stayed inside his room, trying to figure out what to do with himself.

A FEW WEEKS later, Bud fell asleep in front of the television set again, and woke up just in time to get ready for bed. He went into the bedroom and put on his blue striped pajamas and then walked to the bathroom to brush his teeth. He had just put his toothbrush back in the glass, when he happened to look in the mirror and was startled to see some strange old man looking back at him. Who the hell was that guy? Surely not him. Bud looked again and made a face. Oh yes, it was him, all right. Good Lord, when did all that happen?

Peggy had looked at herself in the mirror every day, mostly complaining about something she saw. But like most men, he had never paid much attention to what he looked like . . . until now. What a rude awakening.

After he got into bed, he had to laugh at himself. How shocked he was, seeing how much he had aged. After all, he was almost eighty-four years old. What did he expect? You go along in life thinking old age will never happen to you, and then it does. But what can you do? As he lay there thinking about it, he realized he really didn't care so much about looking good. For whatever time he had left, he just wanted to feel good. But lately his body was not cooperating. Whatever happened to just getting up out of a chair? He'd been forgetting names, and he lost his glasses a lot. But he figured as long as his brain was functioning pretty well and he could still walk, he had a little time left.

He also realized that maybe he should go ahead with a plan he'd made, and sooner rather than later. That old geezer in the bathroom mirror looked like he didn't have a lot more time to spare. He needed to do it now, before it was too late, and just hope he could still pull it off.

Bud got in bed and closed his eyes and, as he often did before going to sleep, he thought about Peggy.

Daddy's Girl

ATLANTA, GEORGIA

2013

RUTHIE HAD PICKED her father up in front of Briarwood Manor and was driving him to the store to get his favorite coffee when he said, "You know, Ruthie, the one thing I really regret about getting older, is that I am sadly unmotorized."

"What?"

"I don't have a car. If I want to go somewhere, I have to call a taxi, or go with a gang of other people on the Briarwood bus. And when I do call a cab, that head guy Merris pokes his snout out of the front office and wants to know where I'm going and what time I'll be back. I feel like a teenage girl."

Ruthie laughed. "Serves you right, Daddy. Do you remember all the times you did the same thing to me? 'Be home by ten,' you'd say."

"Yes, but you really were a teenager. And, by the way, don't think I didn't know all the times you snuck in after ten."

"You did?"

"Yes, I did, and not only that, I always knew where you were and *who* you were with."

"You did not."

"Did, too."

"How?"

"Not telling."

"Okay. But did you know that sometimes I came home before ten, let you hear me come in, and then snuck out the back door?"

Now Bud was surprised. "When?"

"Ha-ha, I have secrets, too."

"Was that when you were dating that idiot Hootie Reynolds?"

Ruthie was surprised. "How did you know I was dating Hootie?"

Bud looked at her. "It was not hard to miss. You had 'Hootie, Hootie, Hootie' written all over your notebook with big kiss marks and hearts. What scared me was when you wrote 'Mrs. Hootie Reynolds' all over the page. It's a good thing you broke up with him, or I would have had to kill him."

Ruthie smiled. "Poor Hootie. He was cute, but he was an idiot, wasn't he? I wonder what would have happened if I had married him."

"You wouldn't have. I would have seen to that. You did just fine in that department. You couldn't have done better than Brooks."

"No, I could not. I still miss him every day, Daddy."

"I know you do, honey. I still miss your mother."

AFTER HE BOUGHT his coffee, and she was driving him back, Ruthie said, "I wonder whatever happened to Hootie."

"I heard he did quite well in sports. Even went to the Olympics."

Ruthie was surprised. "He did? Doing what?"

"Javelin catcher."

"Oh, Daddy. You made that up."

"Yeah, but it could have been true."

. . .

RUTHIE'S HUSBAND, BROOKS, had died suddenly of a heart attack three years earlier. At the time, their two children, Carolyn
and Richard, were still living in Atlanta, and that had helped her
get through it. But then, when Carolyn got married and moved to
Washington, D.C., and Richard and his girlfriend, Dotsie, moved
to Oregon, all Ruthie had left of family living in Atlanta was her
father, and if anything happened to him she didn't know what she
would do. She adored him, and even after all these years, he could
still make her laugh.

The Elephant in the Room

MARTHA LEE HAD never completely accepted Ruthie into the Caldwell family, but that was not the case with her grandchildren, Carolyn and Richard. On the day each child was born, Martha Lee had come swooping into the hospital, dressed to the nines, accepting congratulations from everyone on the birth of her grandchild.

Before they were even born, Martha Lee had already chosen their middle names, the schools they were to attend, and the classes they would be taking. Ballet for Carolyn; tennis, golf, and swimming for Richard. And by royal command, every Sunday and every holiday meal was to be spent with Martha Lee at the club. And while at the club, any introductions to her friends went as follows:

> "You know my son, Brooks, of course, and this is my darling granddaughter, Carolyn Lee, and my handsome grandson, Richard . . . and Brooks's wife."

Ruthie had tried so hard to be civil to Martha Lee for Brooks's and the children's sake, but it was getting harder and harder. Then came Carolyn's wedding.

Ruthie was the mother of the bride. *She* was supposed to oversee her daughter's wedding arrangements. But, as usual, Martha Lee had taken over. The first day Ruthie and Carolyn sat down and started planning, Martha Lee walked over to their house and announced to Ruthie, "Of course we'll use my caterers, and the reception has to be at my house—your yard is far too small. I'll handle the renting of the tents, and the band."

Ruthie had gotten one word in. "But—"

Martha Lee didn't let her finish. "And, Carolyn, I know exactly who we will use to do the invitations. I don't know what date you and Brian were thinking about, but let's not do June. It's so over-done. I'll call All Saints and set a date for the end of May."

A FEW WEEKS later, when Ruthie went with Carolyn to pick out her silver pattern, Carolyn said she needed to ask Grandmother what she thought before the final choice could be made.

As the wedding day drew closer, and everything was being done without her, Ruthie became so frustrated and upset that she pleaded with Carolyn: "I'm your mother. Please, honey, let me do something!"

"Oh, Mother. I don't know why you're making such a fuss. Grandmother wants to do it. All you have to do is show up and look pretty. Grandmother has ordered the most gorgeous wedding cake. She showed me a picture. Wait till you see it, you'll die. We're looking at bridesmaid dresses this afternoon. Grandmother said we have to be very careful with color. She wants something springy, but not too flashy. She said bright colors take attention from the bride. She's thinking a pale lavender, or maybe a blush pink, and for the shoes, she's leaning toward a cream or natural pump. Nothing white, of course." It was no use. It was clear to Ruthie that she was going to be just another guest at her daughter's wedding.

When the day came, Ruthie wore a light beige dress. But, true to form, Martha Lee—going against her own advice—made her grand appearance in a lime-green silk organza dress, with a large hat to match. After all, every occasion was about her . . . wasn't it?

RUTHIE HAD TO admit that as much as she had hoped things would change, they hadn't. Starting at the age of five, if Carolyn was not happy with something at home, she would pack her little bag and march over to Grandmother's house. Of course, Martha Lee was delighted to have her. And it was always the same old battle to get her daughter to come back.

"She's *my* daughter, Martha. She needs to come home."

"Well, she's *my* granddaughter!"

"I understand that, but she's got to learn she can't always get her way."

"Why not? I see no reason she can't have anything she wants. Besides, she told me you were practically starving her to death. No wonder she comes over here."

"Oh, Martha, we are not starving her. She comes to your house because you indulge her. A six-year-old child shouldn't be allowed to eat two and three desserts. All that sugar is not good for her, and while we're on the subject, please don't give her any more wine at dinner. She's way too young to be drinking alcohol."

"I beg to differ. In France all children drink wine."

"Fine, Martha, but we live in Atlanta."

"She's going to have to learn how to choose good wines, sooner or later."

"Well, if you don't mind, I would prefer later, rather than sooner."

This last exchange really threw Martha Lee's nose out of joint and she called Brooks at work. "Your wife is accusing me of turning my only granddaughter into an alcoholic. She absolutely refuses to let her have even one tiny sip of wine with dinner."

Brooks sighed. He had been down this road before. "Mother, please don't give Carolyn wine, and don't put me in the middle of this."

"Well, of all things. There has never been an alcoholic on either side of our families. The very idea is absurd."

Brooks didn't answer, which was his way of letting her know that he was not going to get into a fight over it.

After a moment, Martha Lee said, "I can see that I am being overruled. So per your wife's wishes, your daughter will have no more wine. But let me say this: It's so sad to me that your wife doesn't seem to have the faintest conception of the art of fine dining, something I was trying to impart to Carolyn."

Brooks said nothing again.

After a pause she continued. "Not to tell tales out of school, but when you were out of town last week, I did spot a Little Caesars pizza delivery van leaving your house. Not once, but twice. I think that about says it all."

Brooks hung up and felt tired and torn apart. He didn't know how much more of this he could take. After his father died, he had been under so much pressure, having to take over the company during an economic downturn. The firm was losing money hand over fist. Now he was constantly being put in the middle of his wife and his mother's tug-of-war over how to raise the children. He loved them both. It was hard to continually be forced to take sides. He walked over and poured himself a drink. Ruthie had been right.

They should never have moved into that house in the first place. Living next door to Martha Lee all these years had not been easy. And now with his father gone, the tension between the two women was getting worse. But they were stuck. He couldn't sell the house now.

Nobody knew it, but he'd taken out two extra mortgages on it just to keep the company from going under. And he knew if he lost any of the old original Caldwell homes it would just kill his mother.

What Now?

CALDWELL CIRCLE WAS located in the very center of Tuxedo Park, the most exclusive neighborhood in Atlanta. The Circle was a very large gated and private cul-de-sac consisting of three homes: the original Caldwell home, where Martha Lee lived, and two smaller homes on either side. Ruthie and Brooks's home was on the right and his paternal aunt and her fifth husband lived to the left. Only they were never home. They, as Martha Lee said, "traveled."

Martha Lee liked to point out that the Caldwell family had lived on the Circle for over a hundred years. The original Caldwell, a financier from North Carolina, had settled there in 1898 on a 250-acre tract. Now, the Circle was all that was left of the original Caldwell land.

It was a lovely place to live, with exquisite landscaping and beautiful trees surrounding each home. The problem for Ruthie was that although other homes had been built around it, she felt isolated from the rest of the world. Brooks had been the buffer between herself and Martha Lee. But now that Brooks was gone, Martha Lee didn't even pretend to be nice to Ruthie.

With both her children gone, Ruthie felt lonelier than ever. She wished she could have a cat or a dog for some company, but sadly this was out of the question due to Martha Lee's allergies. She knew she should figure out something to do with her time.

She'd tried taking tango lessons, but the instructor gave her the creeps. Ricardo was evidently always on the rove to marry a rich widow, and as soon as she walked in he'd made a beeline for her. Ricardo didn't know it, but she was not a rich widow. In fact, when Brooks died, she had been surprised to learn just how little money they had left. Their house was mortgaged to the hilt. However, when your name was Caldwell, people just assumed you were wealthy. She was still inundated with requests for donations, and invited to thousand-dollar dinners and five-hundred-dollar luncheons, where she was expected to bid on expensive auction items. Every other call seemed to be someone wanting her to donate something or give money for some charity. She knew Martha Lee would not want it known that any Caldwell had lost most of their money, so she gradually just dropped out of that social circle.

Although she was lonesome, dropping out was in some ways a relief. But she still had a long future in front of her. And filled with what? She was no longer a wife or a mother, both her children were grown and married. So who was she?

She should have finished college. She remembered how much she'd wanted to become an interior designer. She had even taken a theater course in college and had been very good at set decoration. But while she had been busy raising her children, the world had left her behind. Unless you were computer savvy, you didn't stand a chance at getting a good job. And where modern technology was concerned, Ruthie was still somewhat in the dark ages. Her doctor had prescribed some kind of antidepressant pills, but they gave her anxiety, so she stopped taking them. She would rather feel depressed than anxious.

She was at a crossroads. She either had to turn left or right, or sit in the same old place and wait until it was her time to move on to Briarwood Manor, or, as her father called it, "God's little waiting room."

The Weems Weekly

(WHISTLE STOP, ALABAMA'S WEEKLY BULLETIN)
April 28, 1954

BEAUTY SHOP TO CLOSE

Opal Butts tells me that since most of her customers were railroad wives, and so due to a lack of paying customers, she is going to have to close down the beauty shop and move to over to Birmingham. Sign of the times, I guess. I remember when I was growing up, there were thirty or more trains coming through a day, now there are maybe only four or five. Sheriff Grady says it's partly because people are in too big a hurry to get somewhere and are jumping on airplanes instead of taking the train. As for me, I told Wilbur that I wouldn't ride up in the air in one of those flying tin cans for all the tea in China.

Idgie Threadgoode says that business is down at the cafe, too. I sure hope she can hang on. What would we do without the cafe? Here's hoping one of those super-duper highways they're talking about will come out our way and bring a whole lot of new folks to town.

On a happier note: Idgie tells me that her brother Julian has now moved from Marianna, Florida, to Kissimmee and has purchased a two-acre orange grove. Also heard from Idgie that Buddy Threadgoode is still in the top five of his class at college and plans on becoming a veterinarian. And another little birdie (Peggy's mother) tells me that wedding bells for Buddy and Peggy might be ringing real soon. As we all know, Buddy did not have a good beginning in life, but it sure looks like he is going to have a happy ending.

As of this week I am running out of news, so if you have any, bring it over. Make it good news if you can. We need all we can get.

. . . Dot Weems . . .

P.S. Here IS an interesting post office fact for you: Did you know that up until 1913, children in America could legally be sent by parcel post? Whew. I'm glad I wasn't a postmistress then!

Briarwood Manor

ATLANTA, GEORGIA

December 2013

THE YOUNGISH WOMAN with slightly pink skin and red fuzzy hair quickly adjusted her glasses as she scanned through the contacts file in Mr. Merris's computer.

A clearly distraught Mr. Merris had just rushed into her office with the news, and ordered her to call Mr. Threadgoode's daughter "right now" and let her know. Then he'd run back out, leaving her holding the ball. When she reached the names starting with the letter "C," she suddenly felt a sense of dread. Oh Lord, she wished she'd never taken this job. She'd only been working at Briarwood for three months and already regretted it. If she hadn't just bought herself a new Toyota hatchback, she would have quit the very first week. The job was just too emotionally draining. She was perfectly fine doing accounting and filling out payroll, but she hated having to deal directly with the families, particularly when she had to be the bearer of bad news. And why did Mr. Merris need her to call the daughter "right now"? Why didn't he just wait and make the call himself? He was good at it, and was used to it. She wasn't.

After she found the name and number, she took a deep breath and dialed. She could already feel the perspiration beginning to form on her upper lip. "Oh, please, let it be an answering machine so I can leave a message." But, unfortunately, after three rings a live person answered.

"Hello?"

"Is this Mrs. Brooks Caldwell?"

"Yes, it is," said a pleasant voice.

"Uh . . . Mrs. Caldwell, this is Janice Poole, assistant director at Briarwood Manor. We met the last time you were here, in the reception area. . . . I have red hair?"

"Oh, yes. How are you?"

"Well, um, not so great at the moment. I am so sorry to have to tell you this, but I'm afraid we lost your father this morning."

"What? . . . Oh no . . ."

"Mr. Merris wanted me to call you right away and let you know."

Ruthie, who had been standing by her kitchen sink having a last sip of iced tea, suddenly felt weak. She walked over to the table and sat down.

"Mrs. Caldwell? Are you still there?"

"Yes, I'm here. . . . Oh my God."

"I'm so so sorry."

"Oh my God . . . what happened? I just talked to him last night."

"He didn't say, all I know is Mr. Merris seemed extremely upset and said it happened under very unusual circumstances, and to tell you that he will be calling you within the hour with the exact details."

"You don't know the details?"

"No, I'm so sorry. . . . I don't."

"Where is my father now?"

"I don't know."

"Oh . . . well . . . can't Mr. Merris come to the phone now?"

Janice looked out her door and saw that Mr. Merris was still outside on the sidewalk talking to the policeman.

"He's still tied up dealing with the authorities right now. But I'm sure he will call just as soon as he can. And again, I am so very sorry. . . ."

After she hung up, Janice looked out the window again. Something odd was definitely going on. She'd never seen Mr. Merris so upset. And why had he called the police? That was definitely weird. Did he suspect some sort of foul play?

Losing Daddy

AFTER SHE HUNG up, Ruthie felt as though she had been hit in the stomach with a shovel. Then when the initial jolt wore off, and the news started to sink in, she began to feel an all-too-familiar numbing sensation. Having been through this situation twice before, she realized that she was probably going into shock. Sadly, she was no stranger to this kind of life-shattering news.

A few months ago, she had received the same phone call from Mr. Merris, telling her that her mother had suddenly passed away. And three years before that, a mutual friend had called and told her that Brooks, her forty-eight-year-old husband and the love of her life, had just dropped dead on the golf course. And like today, both calls had come from completely out of the blue. Of course, she'd known this call would be coming someday, but no matter what you thought, you were never really prepared.

Ruthie could feel her heart pounding and her hands were shaky. She glanced up at the clock. It was almost twelve noon. What should she do? Should she call her son and her daughter? Or should she just wait to hear from Mr. Merris? No, she wouldn't call. She would wait until she had more . . . information. The girl said it had happened that morning. Then she wondered why they'd waited so long to call her. That didn't sound like he had died in his sleep. Was he still in his room? Had it been some kind of accident? She wouldn't doubt it. Lately he had been so stubborn, and refused to wear his new arm except for special occasions, which only made it worse when he fell. He'd fallen and broken his wrist the last time. She sighed. After spending all that money, time, and energy to get the very best prosthetic arm made, why wouldn't he just wear it? Ruthie was suddenly torn between being mad at him and heartbroken at the same time.

It had been ten minutes. Should she go ahead and just call Mr. Merris? Or wait for him to call back? Oh Lord . . . she looked at the clock again. "What's taking him so long?"

What had happened? And what authorities was Mr. Merris talking to?

The more time she had to think about it, the more she was convinced it must have been some kind of accident. A few years ago, a resident at the Manor had walked through a crosswalk without looking, and a truck had backed up and hit him. The poor man was so deaf he hadn't heard the beeping. But that couldn't have been the case with her daddy. He could hear, and he could see perfectly fine. He had just had his cataract operation a few years earlier. He'd had a new hip put in four years ago, and a top-of-the-line hearing aid. He'd been patched up as well as one could be at almost eighty-four. And it couldn't have been a heart attack; they had just put in a pacemaker. Besides, Miss Poole had just said that whatever happened, had happened under "unusual" circumstances. What did she mean by unusual? He must have fallen. But falling wasn't that unusual for people in their eighties. He fell all the time. Maybe this time he fell and hit his head on something. Oh no. She hoped he hadn't suffered.

She looked up at the clock again.

Why hadn't she gone out to see him last Wednesday? Why did she go to that stupid beauty makeover that day? Oh God, as usual, no matter how much you'd done for the person when they were alive, you'd forget the good, and the regrets would start marching in.

What should she do next, she wondered. Thank heavens he had written down his life history for her. She would make copies of it and give it to the kids. At least they would have that. . . . Poor Daddy. He was so good. She had hoped to have more time with him.

There were so many more things she wished she'd asked him. Now it was too late.

Nervous in the Service

MR. MERRIS STOOD out on the sidewalk wringing his hands, his dark brown toupee listing a little more toward his left eye than usual.

He and a few members of his staff were talking to a police officer, who was busy asking questions and taking down notes.

"Can you tell me what he was wearing when last seen?"

Mr. Merris turned to the bus driver. "Jerome, you saw him last. Do you remember?"

"Uh . . . khaki pants, and some sort of old tweed or plaid wool jacket. Red or green tie, maybe?"

As the policeman wrote down the description, a breathless young woman ran out of the building and handed him a photograph.

"This is the most recent one we have on file."

The policeman took it and looked at it for a moment, then casually attached it to the top of his clipboard.

Mr. Merris, who was growing more frantic by the moment said, "Listen, officer . . . couldn't you just go and find him? Do we really need to waste all this time filling out a report? I mean, how long does someone have to be missing before they are declared missing? As you can see, he's a very old man, and I'm extremely concerned about his welfare."

The officer looked at the photograph once again. "You say he has an arm missing?"

Mr. Merris nodded. "Yes . . . Well, sometimes."

The officer looked up at him quizzically.

"He has a prosthesis."

"A what?" asked the officer.

"An artificial arm."

"Ahh . . . I see. Left or right?"

"Pardon?"

"Left or right arm?"

"Oh."

Mr. Merris was unsure and turned to the nurse, who answered "Left."

Mr. Merris repeated, "Left. Only sometimes he doesn't wear it."

The nurse added, "He always wears it on special occasions, though."

The officer wrote on his report *May or may not have a left arm.* "So . . . would you say he is in ill health? Frail?"

"No, no. Not frail," Mr. Merris said. "But he's still an at-risk senior, missing for over six hours now. Not to mention that Mr. Threadgoode is also a member of a very prominent family."

The officer looked up from his pad unfazed. "Is he an Alzheimer's patient?"

Mr. Merris shook his head. "No, a little dementia perhaps." The nurse nodded in agreement. "Maybe, just a little, but he's certainly able to function."

"Has he been depressed lately . . . any threats of suicide?"

"Oh no, nothing like that," said Mr. Merris. "Mr. Threadgoode is more"—he turned to the activities director for help—"what would you say, Hattie? Upbeat?"

"Yes, he's kind of a jokester, really. He's very funny. Just last week he—"

Mr. Merris interrupted, "I just don't understand how this

could have happened, Officer. All the shuttle bus drivers at Briar-wood are highly trained. They have strict rules to *never, ever* leave the parking lot until all the residents on the bus have been accounted for. But as I said before, the minute we realized Mr. Threadgoode was missing, Jerome immediately turned around and drove back to the church, but he was gone."

Jerome confirmed. "I looked everywhere . . . checked the bathrooms and everything."

The policeman flipped his pad shut and said, "Okeydokey, I think I have enough, so I'll go ahead and issue a BOLO on him."

"A what?" asked Mr. Merris, somewhat alarmed.

"Be on the Lookout alert."

"Oh . . . well, good. . . . And then what?"

"Then we hope we find him."

Why Isn't He Calling?

RUTHIE LOOKED AT the clock. It had been over twenty-five minutes. Why wasn't he calling? Should she just get in the car and go over there? What should she do? She felt so helpless. She had assumed that when this day did come, Brooks would be there by her side helping her, taking care of everything like he always did. Then it suddenly hit her. Now that Brooks and Daddy were both gone, she didn't have anybody to turn to for help. She'd never felt so alone in her life.

A few years ago, the family lawyer had said that all of her father's papers were in order, but she didn't know any of the particulars. The only thing her father had told her was that when he passed away, she had a surprise coming. Lord only knows what it was. He was so silly. Always doing silly things, just to make you laugh.

At this point, she wasn't sure how much money her father had left. She knew before her parents moved to Briarwood, he had spent a fortune on doctors and caregivers for her mother. But she really didn't care. It was his to do with whatever he liked. He had worked hard all his life and had earned every penny.

She looked at the clock again.

Oh God. If she had it to do over, after her mother died, she would have insisted that he move in with her where she could have kept an eye on him. But on the other hand, he'd seemed to like it at the Manor. And he had made a lot of friends. If she had moved him in with her, her mother-in-law wouldn't have been very nice to him.

She looked at the clock again. Why wasn't Mr. Merris calling?

She dreaded telling the kids. She knew they would both be upset. She wondered if she should plan some service, or something.

She did know that he wanted to be buried in Whistle Stop in the Threadgoode family plot. She knew that. But she didn't really know where the Whistle Stop cemetery was, or if it was even still there anymore. Then something else occurred to her. With Daddy gone, she was the last living Threadgoode.

The Escapee

BUD THREADGOODE HAD had a hunch the new bus driver was not very sharp. And since he was now seven miles away from Briarwood Manor, sitting in the Waffle House across the street from the Atlanta train station, he figured his assessment had been correct.

Earlier that morning, after the small white bus with BRIARWOOD MANOR DISTINCTIVE SENIOR LIVING written on the side pulled out of the Baptist church parking lot, Bud had come out of the church bathroom where he had been hiding. He'd looked out and saw that the bus was not coming back looking for him, and hightailed it over to the big Catholic church a few blocks away. He needed to find someone who would call a cab to pick him up and take him to the train station. Ruthie had just bought him a new Jitterbug cellphone, and Bud's one big slipup was that he had been in such a hurry this morning, he'd left it on his dresser. But luckily, when he got there, people were still milling around the Catholic church parking lot. He asked a nice Mexican family who were just leaving if they would call him a cab, and the father said they would be happy to drive him. When they let him out across the street from the train station, he tried to pay them for the ride, but they wouldn't take it. Instead, the tiny little grandmother in the back seat handed him an "Our Lady of Guadalupe" holy card, and he was glad to have it. With what he had planned to do, he needed all the help he could get.

He wasn't trying to upset anybody or disappear for good. All he wanted to do was take a ride on the train. It wasn't a spur-of-the-moment thing. He had been planning today's little caper for quite a while. For the last few months, he had been taking different church shuttle buses every other Sunday just to confuse the Briar-wood staff.

He had managed to look up the train schedule, and last Friday, he had slipped into the new assistant's office while she was at lunch and printed out a round-trip ticket. He was taking the Amtrak train from Atlanta to Birmingham, then coming back to Atlanta on the same day. Hopefully, he'd be back at the Manor in time for dinner. If all went well, they wouldn't even know he was gone. He certainly didn't want to upset Ruthie; she had enough troubles without worrying about him.

He had been looking so forward to making this trip again. When he was a kid, Aunt Idgie had been friends with all the railroad men in Whistle Stop, and knowing how much he loved trains, the engineers used to let him ride with them over to Atlanta and back. His mother was not too happy about it, but had let him go, as long as he was home by dark. What fun those trips were. The engineers let him blow the whistle at all the crossings. And on the way back home, the Pullman porter on the Crescent always brought him a ham and cheese sandwich and a big silver bowl of vanilla ice cream from the dining car. How lucky can a kid get?

All he wanted to do was ride the train past Whistle Stop one more time. He had heard there was really nothing much left. But he still wanted to see it.

Time on My Hands

As Bud found his platform and waited for the train, he felt sad and happy at the same time. He'd wanted to make this trip while he was still in his right mind and in fairly good physical health. He was slipping just a bit, and he knew it. Just this morning he had walked out and forgotten his phone. This could be his last trip back to Alabama for all he knew.

For years, Bud had sworn up and down that he would never be one of those old codgers sitting around all day talking about the past. But lately, God help him, the past had been on his mind a lot. He had to admit he was now a card-carrying member of the "Back when I was a boy" club.

After he boarded the long Amtrak train to Birmingham, Bud made his way down the aisle and noticed an empty seat next to a nice-looking young person. He had to look twice because the person had their hair pulled back in some kind of bun. But as he got closer, he saw it was a boy.

"Pardon me, son, is this seat taken?" he asked.

"No sir, please sit down."

"Thank you."

After he sat down, Bud asked him, "Where are you traveling today? Going down to New Orleans?"

"No sir. Going home to Birmingham."

"Ah . . . me too."

"Oh are you from Birmingham, too?"

"No, but close. I'm from a little place right outside you've probably never heard of called Whistle Stop."

The young man said, "Whistle Stop? Gosh, I think I remember my grandmother saying something about riding through a town called Whistle Stop."

"Is that right?"

"Yes sir. My grandparents used to take the train to New York every year to do Christmas shopping."

"Well, Whistle Stop's the place where I grew up, but like a lot of things, it's not there anymore. Things change, time marches on."

The boy looked sympathetic. "I know just how you feel. My old neighborhood has changed a lot since I was young."

"I see. . . . If you don't mind me asking, how old are you, son?"

"Twenty-two."

"Lucky you. Twenty-two is a great age." Then Bud laughed. "Come to think of it, every age is a great age. At least that's been my experience. Some are better than others, but every year has something good to offer. What's your name?"

"William Hornbeck, Jr. But people call me Billy."

"Well, happy to meet you, Billy. My name is Bud Threadgoode. I'm going to be eighty-four years old next week."

"Wow. What's that like, to be eighty-four?"

"I don't know yet, but I can tell you what the best part of being eighty-three is."

"What's that, sir?"

"No more peer pressure." Buddy looked over at him and grinned, and the young man laughed.

"I guess that would be great, all right. I'm in grad school over at Emory. It's a lot of pressure."

"Is that so? What are you studying?"

"Applied sociology."

Bud nodded. "Well, I don't have any idea what that is, but it sounds like you must be a pretty smart fellow. I'm a retired person myself."

Bud pulled out his old brown leather wallet and opened it up.

"Here's a picture of my daughter, Ruthie, when she was six . . . and this one is when she was homecoming queen."

"Wow, she was a beauty."

Bud smiled. "Thank you. She still is. Here she is with my two grandchildren. She lost her husband a few years ago. It was hard but she picked up the ball and went on. I'm so proud of her, I don't know what I'd do without her. Best daughter in the world. Calls me every day. I just talked to her this morning. . . . Of course, I didn't tell where I was headed today."

"Is she your only child?"

"Yep, and I sure hit the jackpot with her."

Billy said, "I'm an only child."

"Well, I'll be dogged. Here we've just met and already we have something in common. I am, too. I kinda liked being the only one, but it can be hard on some folks. Ruthie's husband was an only child, and it came with an awful lot of responsibility. Too much, if you ask me. That's why I don't tell Ruthie a lot of things. Don't want to worry her too much."

"By the way, that's a very cool jacket you have on."

"Why, thank you. My wife bought it for me. I've had it since 1959, but it's still good as new, don't you think?"

"Yes sir. If you don't mind my asking, Mr. Threadgoode, what was your line of business?"

"Not at all. I was a doctor of veterinary medicine."

"A veterinarian. Oh cool. . . . Did you always want to be a vet?"

Bud nodded. "Pretty much. And I guess I can blame my Aunt Idgie for that. She was a big animal lover. From the time I can remember, she always had a couple of cats, and took in every stray animal for miles around. Some of them so sick or hurt they were barely alive. But somehow she was able to nurse them back to life. Possums, birds, baby squirrels, you name it. One time somebody brought her a chicken that had lost both its feet in an accident, and darned if she didn't figure out a way to make it a pair of new feet."

"How'd she do that?

"She took a pair of leather baby shoes and glued them on its legs, and before you knew it that chicken was running all over the yard in pink leather baby shoes."

"Really?"

"Oh yeah, and when one shoe came off, she'd just glue another one on. We even had an alligator once, with half his tail missing."

"An alligator?"

"Sure did. My uncle Julian was living down in Florida at the time and found it on the side of the road and brought it to her. She kept it in a big cement tub in the back of the cafe, with wires over the top, so it wouldn't escape."

"Was it dangerous?"

"Oh, you bet he was. One time he got loose and was hiding under the steps. And the next morning when I came down them headed for school he jumped out and bit the hell out of me."

"No . . ."

"Oh yeah, just about took my whole leg off."

Billy was horrified. "Oh no . . . your whole leg?"

Bud smiled. "Well . . . it was more like a toe. Makes a good story though, doesn't it?"

Billy said, "Yeah, an alligator . . . wow."

Bud smiled. He was going to have a good time with this boy.

Briarwood Manor

ATLANTA, GEORGIA

As THEY STOOD and watched the police car drive away, Mr. Merris turned to the nervous bus driver. "I'm telling you, Jerome, if anything happens to Mr. Threadgoode and that family sues us . . . I've a good mind to have you drug tested."

Jerome's eyes suddenly opened up very wide. He wasn't a doper, but he did smoke a little pot now and then.

Mr. Merris looked at him and said, "No, on second thought, I'd better not. If we found something, then we would be liable for sure. What I don't understand is why you didn't check your list before you left the lot."

"I did, Mr. Merris. And I swear he wasn't on the list."

"And what was he doing on the Baptist bus? He should have been on the Methodist bus."

Mr. Merris turned to the activities director who had been standing nearby on the sidewalk. "Hattie, you were there when they were boarding, what do you know about Mr. Threadgoode being on the Baptist bus?"

"Well . . . a couple of months ago, I do remember he got on the Presbyterian bus, and last week he took the Unity bus. And the week before, I think it might have been the Christian Scientist bus, but he always signed in, until today."

"Why was he doing all that church hopping?"

Hattie shrugged. "He told me he was a spiritual seeker."

"Oh, great," Mr. Merris sniffed. "Well, thanks to you two, unless he shows up soon, we all may be new *job* seekers."

As they all followed Mr. Merris back into the building, Hattie's friend who worked in the dining room caught up with Hattie and walked beside her.

"What's going on?" she whispered.

"Mr. Threadgoode escaped."

"Really?"

"Yep. Flew the coop."

"When?"

"This morning"

"Good for him."

"Yeah. And Mr. Merris is having a fit."

The Mix-up

YES, MR. MERRIS *was* having a fit, and he thought with good reason. Naturally, they'd had residents wander away from the Manor before. With a large memory care unit on the premises, it was to be expected. But in the past, they had always been found within the hour, somewhere on the property. Mr. Threadgoode had been missing for over three and a half hours now, and this could very well mean Mr. Merris's job. Not only had they lost a resident under his watch, it was the particular resident they'd lost that was so worrisome.

Richard Merris had started his professional life as choir director at the large All Saints Episcopal Church on Peachtree. It was the church all the old established monied families of Atlanta attended. And when their time came, Briarwood Manor was *the* preferred retirement home.

Eleven years ago, when Mrs. Sockwell, the former director of operations at Briarwood Manor, had what was later described as "a small nervous breakdown," it was Mr. Merris's good fortune to have been personally recommended for the position by none other than Mrs. Martha Lee Caldwell. Not only was she a lifetime board member at Briarwood, but her husband's parents had been founding members. The elder Caldwells had donated the land, the building, and all the artwork that now graced the walls. Granted, Mr. Threadgoode wasn't a Caldwell; he was the father of Martha's daughter-in-law. But even so, Mr. Merris didn't want to rile Martha Lee for any reason. He knew that if anything bad happened to Mr. Threadgoode, he was toast. Burnt toast.

MR. MERRIS WALKED back into his office, sat down at his desk, took his roll of Tums from his drawer, and then buzzed Miss Poole.

"Did you call the daughter?"

"Yes sir."

"Listen, when you spoke to her, you didn't sound too concerned, did you? I think we need to downplay this as much as we can, for as long as we can."

"I just told her what you said to say, that we lost her father and you would be calling later with the details."

"Okay. And did you say anything else?"

"No sir. I didn't know anything else to say."

"All right then. I'd better get this over with. I just hope to God she hasn't called her mother-in-law yet."

Mr. Merris glanced at himself in the mirror, adjusted his toupee a little to the right, and prepared himself for what could be a difficult phone call. He needed to sound as casual as he could under the circumstances. "Just put a smile in your voice," he said, "and be calm." He smiled and dialed. Ruthie picked up on the first ring.

"Hello?"

"Mrs. Caldwell," he oozed, "Richard Merris here. How are you doing? Listen, dear, I know Miss Poole called and told you a little bit about what was going on."

"Yes . . . she did."

"I hated to bother you with this, but frankly, Mrs. Caldwell, I really don't think it's all that serious. I know, it's a little disconcerting not knowing where he is at the moment, but I'll bet one day, we'll all be laughing about it."

Ruthie sat there wondering if she had suddenly gone insane or if he had.

"Mr. Merris . . . I don't understand. Why would I ever be laughing about the loss of my father?"

"Oh no. I meant no offense. No, I just meant when we do locate him, and he's perfectly fine, we'll laugh about having been so worried, that's all. And technically, we didn't actually lose him. He just got off the Briarwood bus and walked away."

"What?"

"Yes, and I was just informed by my staff that for some time now, every Sunday, your father has been getting on the wrong bus, and I hate to say it, Mrs. Caldwell, but quite frankly, I'm beginning to think it was all a ruse, and this . . . um . . . little stunt was planned all along and not an oversight on our part. But having said that, I can assure you that everything that can be done is being done."

By now Ruthie's head was spinning

"Wait . . . wait a minute. What bus? I'm so confused. Isn't my father dead?"

Mr. Merris's heart almost stopped. "Dead? Have you heard something? Has someone called you?"

"Yes, Miss Poole called and said my father had died this morning."

"What? She said your father was *dead*?"

"I thought that's what she said."

"Your father's not dead. He's just missing. Oh my heavenly Lord, can you give me a moment, Mrs. Caldwell?" He put his hand over the receiver and yelled into the next office. "Miss Poole,

GET IN HERE . . . RIGHT THIS MINUTE! Mrs. Caldwell, let me call you right back. I have to fire someone."

Janice Poole, who had seen this coming for some time, had already quietly packed her few personal things in a box and was on her way out the door. The hell with the Toyota hatchback; she'd get a bicycle.

AFTER SHE HUNG up with Mr. Merris, Ruthie broke down and sobbed. She had just been through one of the worst hours of her life. She had her father dead and buried and now, to suddenly find out he was alive. All the emotions of relief came flooding out. Thank goodness she hadn't called the children and upset them for no reason. Daddy was alive. All that worry for nothing. Then it slowly started to sink in. Yes, he was alive, but, according to Mr. Merris, he was still missing. Oh Lord. Now she didn't know if she should be worried about him anymore or not. Her father had a history of doing silly things. And if disappearing like this turned out to be one of his little jokes, when he did show up, she was going to kill him.

Amtrak

CAR 6
Seats 11 and 12

BUD THREADGOODE AND Billy Hornbeck were now deep in conversation. Billy was quite impressed that Bud had been a veterinarian and wanted to hear more about it, and Bud was perfectly happy holding court, telling him about some of his experiences.

"Of course, I was lucky," he said. "In my profession, I mostly dealt with nice people. But I met a few bad apples along the way. You know, Billy, you can tell a lot about a person by the way they treat their animals. I like just about everybody, and I can forgive a lot of things. But I don't have a bit of use for a person who will mistreat an animal. My Aunt Idgie was the same way. One time, somebody threatened to kill her cat. And back then there was no animal control or anybody you could call. You had to take matters into your own hands."

"Did she?"

"Oh yes. And she nearly went to jail over it, too."

"Really?"

"It all started when this guy named Arvel Ligget from Pell City kept coming over to Whistle Stop and pestering all the women in town, leering at young girls, things like that. A real bad guy. Anyhow, he was always coming into the cafe and hanging around, but one day, when he was sitting at the counter, he started making lewd remarks to my mother. And before he knew it, Aunt Idgie had come around the counter, grabbed him by the collar, and thrown him out the door, and told him to never come back."

"For real?"

"Oh yeah, so after she threw him out like that, Arvel got real mad. He'd seen Aunt Idgie's big white cat coming in and out of the cafe, and he told somebody that the first chance he got, he was going to go back over there and kill it, to get even with her. And oh boy, when Aunt Idgie heard what he'd threatened to do, she jumped in her car and drove over to Pell City and found him in the pool hall. She went in and told him that if he ever came within twenty-five feet of the cafe or her cat, she'd shoot him."

"Wow . . . did he ever come back?"

"Oh yeah, he came back all right."

"What happened?"

"Well, I was pretty young at the time, but I remember that night very well. And when that shotgun blast went off, it sure scared the hell out of me, I'll tell you that."

Whistle Stop, Alabama

1933

A LOT OF guys at the pool hall over in Pell City had heard Idgie yelling at Arvel that day, which had made him even madder. He wasn't going to get scared off or ordered around by some damn female. That cat was as good as dead.

A few weeks later, it was around three A.M. when Arvel, carrying a baseball bat and a knife, came sneaking up to the back of the cafe. He walked very slowly past the garden and the chicken coop. And as he got closer to the back of the cafe, he could see Idgie's big white cat in the moonlight, sleeping on the top steps. As he crept quietly closer and closer, he began to whisper ever so softly, "Here, Kitty, Kitty."

The moment Idgie heard her chickens clucking, she sat up in bed. After she heard them again, she got up and went to the window. She pulled back a corner of the curtain just in time to see Arvel Ligget creeping toward the cafe. She then quietly tiptoed over to the loaded twenty-gauge shotgun she kept by the door, and picked it up. She waited until she figured he was twenty-five feet away, give or take a foot or two, then she kicked open the back door and yelled, "Run for your life, you Son of a Bitch!" She counted to three and then pulled the trigger. After the sudden loud blast, Ruth sat straight up in bed and screamed, Buddy started crying, and all the dogs in town started barking. Soon, all hell broke loose. Lights went on in every house, and people started running out into their yards in their nightclothes, wondering what had happened.

A few hours later, just as the sun was coming up, Sheriff Grady Kilgore drove up to the back of the cafe, where Idgie and Ruth were waiting. Idgie was now out of her nightshirt, fully dressed, expecting to be arrested and go to jail. Buddy was scared and holding on to her, and Ruth was in tears.

When Grady walked in, Idgie looked at him.

"Well . . . did I kill him?"

Grady sat down at the table and pushed his hat back on his head. "Naw . . . you didn't kill him."

"Oh, thank heavens," said a relieved Ruth.

"But he's still over at the hospital. The last time I saw him they were still picking a load of buckshot out of him. What in the hell were you aiming at, Idgie?"

"His backside, why?"

"Well, he must have turned around, because that's sure as hell not where you hit him."

"Where did I hit him?"

Grady laughed. "Let's put it this way, I don't think he'll be fooling around with any more ladies for a while. Maybe never, the way he's carrying on. Give me a cup of that coffee, will you, Ruth? A little cream no sugar."

"Is he gonna press charges against me?" asked Idgie.

"Oh, he was, but I explained it would be best if he didn't."

Ruth poured his coffee and handed it to him.

"Thanks, Ruth. I think I convinced him that it might be better for him if he just went on back to Pell City and to not be comin' over here anymore. I told him I couldn't guarantee his safety if he did."

"What did he say?"

"He said you were a crazy woman that should be locked up for the good of the community."

"What did you say?"

"I agreed."

Just then the white cat with one eye walked in, jumped up on the table, and started trying to drink Grady's coffee. Grady quickly grabbed his cup away, looked at the cat, and said, "I tell you what, you sure are one lucky cat. Because if Ligget had caught you last night, you would have been one dead cat today." Grady took a last sip of coffee and stood up. "Well, I gotta go fill out my report . . . accidental shooting."

A much-relieved Ruth said, "Thank you, Grady."

"You're welcome."

He went to the door and then turned around and said, "Idgie, do me a favor, will you?"

"Of course, Grady, anything."

"If you ever go to shoot me, give me fair warning first, so I can turn around, okay?"

SHERIFF GRADY KILGORE had known Idgie since they were kids, and he'd seen her almost every day of his life. After he was grown, he'd eaten at the cafe more often than home, which suited Gladys Kilgore just fine. Less cooking for her. But after he had left that morning, Grady was glad that Idgie'd had a little scare, thinking she was going to jail. She was way too wild and reckless for her own good. Everybody in town knew that Ruth had left her once over her drinking and gambling down at the River Club. If Idgie wasn't careful, one of these days she might do something else crazy, and get herself in some real trouble. Trouble he couldn't get her out of. But for now, there was no way that he was going to let Arvel Ligget press any charges against her. He hadn't told Idgie this, because he didn't want to encourage her to shoot more people, but Ligget had it coming. Anybody that would try and kill a poor little kitty cat had it coming. Grady was six-foot-four and looked tough, but he had a tender heart.

ARVEL LIGGET NEVER did come back to the town of Whistle Stop. He was too afraid of Sheriff Kilgore. But that day he made a vow that if he ever caught Idgie Threadgoode anywhere outside of town, he'd make her pay for what she had done.

Aboard the Amtrak

CAR 6
Seats 11 and 12

LATER, WHEN BOTH of them decided they were hungry, Bud and Billy went to the snack bar and came back with prepackaged ham and cheese sandwiches wrapped in cellophane. Bud hadn't ridden the train in a long time, and that tiny little snack bar was a far cry from the lovely old formal dining cars the trains used to have. But he didn't say anything. He just ordered the ham and cheese and a Coke.

As THEY ATE lunch, Bud told Billy the story of how he'd lost his arm and his Aunt Idgie had nicknamed him Stump. "I was down about it and having a pretty hard time. She said it was better for me to call myself Stump before anybody else did." Bud laughed. "She even threw a funeral for my arm. And I went by Stump for quite a while, till my mother put a stop to it. My mother was real proper, but Aunt Idgie didn't have a proper bone in her body. She was always telling jokes and acting a fool. Everybody knew if you needed a good laugh, she was always up for a good time and always full of fun."

By now the train was almost halfway to Birmingham. "It sure

sounds like you must have had a lot of fun growing up at that cafe," Billy said.

Bud smiled. "I did. I knew all the railroad men. They'd all come in for breakfast. Everybody in town ate there. But we also had a lot of people who'd heard about the place, and you never knew who was liable to walk in on any given day. Yeah, I met a lot of interesting people there. And one pretty interesting dummy, too."

"Who was that?"

Bud laughed. "Well that's a long story."

"I'd sure like to hear it," said Billy, biting into his sandwich.

Whistle Stop, Alabama

1937

ONE HOT, MUGGY August afternoon, a dark green Packard with a cardboard placard on the back that read THE OATMAN FAMILY SINGERS TRAVELING FOR JESUS slowly pulled up to the front of the cafe. A few minutes later, a large woman wiggled her way out of the back seat and walked up to the screen door of the cafe, threw it open, stepped inside, and announced in a loud voice, "It's Minnie Oatman! I'm here to get me some of them famous fried green tomatoes. Am I at the right place?"

A startled Ruth looked up at the woman who was as wide as the door she'd just entered, and was speechless. But Idgie, who had seen Minnie's picture on a poster on a telephone pole over in Gate City, recognized her right away, and said, "You sure are, Mrs. Oatman. Come on in."

"Oh good. Me and the boys was doin' an all-night gospel sing over in Gate City and I told my husband, Ferris, I said, I'm not leaving Alabama till I get me some."

Minnie waddled over to the counter and looked at the stools.

"Honey, you're gonna have to charge me twice. I cain't fit on that one little bitty stool." She then heaved herself up and sat down on two stools and asked Idgie, "What's your name, hon?"

"I'm Idgie, and this is Ruth."

"Well, hey, glad to know you. I left the boys sleeping in the car.

They'd rather sleep than eat. Not me. I want me a plate of fried green tomatoes and some sweet tea." Sipsey peeked out over the double doors to the kitchen and snuck a look at Minnie. Minnie saw her and called out, "Is that Sipsey Peavey I see?"

Sipsey said, "Yes'm."

"Well, gal, that woman who told me about this place said you are the best cook in Alabama. Is that right?"

Sipsey giggled. "Yes'm."

Just as Minnie was ordering another dozen fried green tomatoes and a half of a coconut cake to go, seven-year-old Buddy Threadgoode walked through the cafe on his way back to his room. As he went by, Idgie grabbed him by the back of his shirt. "Whoa . . . stop. I want to introduce you to somebody. Buddy, this is Mrs. Oatman, and she and her family are famous gospel singers."

Buddy's eyes got wide. He had never seen anybody that fat before.

"Well, hey there, Buddy," said Minnie. Then looked at him and asked, "Where's your little arm, honey?"

Ruth jumped in. "He had an accident, Mrs. Oatman."

Minnie made a sad face and said, "Aww, ain't that too bad. . . . Well, the good Lord giveth and he taketh away. How old are you, little Buddy?"

Buddy managed a weak reply. "Seven."

"Seven? Well ain't that something. I got somebody out in the car who would just love to meet you."

She looked at Idgie, "Honey, run out there and wake Floyd up and tell him to bring Chester in here. I got somebody I want him to meet."

A few minutes later, a disheveled-looking man walked in the door carrying a small wooden ventriloquist dummy with red wooden lips and painted freckles, wearing a blond wig and dressed in a small red cowboy suit and red cowboy hat. He was known professionally as Chester, the only scripture-quoting, gospel-singing dummy in the world.

Minnie said, "Chester, this here is Buddy. . . . Say hello."

Chester suddenly sprang to life. He looked at Buddy, blinked his eyes, and shot his eyebrows up and down, and said, "Hello there, Buddy. How are you?"

Buddy's jaw dropped. He had never seen anything like this in his life. "I'm fine," he said, barely audibly.

Chester said, "How old are you, Buddy?"

"Seven."

"Whoo-whee. Me, too! Would you like to be my friend?"

Buddy nodded. "Yes."

"Great!" Let's shake on it." Chester stuck out his small wooden hand, and Buddy shook it.

Then Minnie said, "Hey, Chester. Why don't you sing Buddy a little song?"

Chester said cheerfully, "Okay, Minnie!" Then Chester looked up at Floyd. "Hey, Floyd. What song should I sing?"

Floyd shrugged and then said, "How about 'Ridin' the Range for Jesus'? Or, 'When It's Round-Up Time Up Yonder'?"

Chester looked at Buddy. "Which one would you like to hear?"

"Umm . . . I guess, the round-up one?"

"Good choice, Buddy, one of my favorites." Minnie then got up and walked over to the old stand-up piano in the corner and sat down and played, while Chester sang and yodeled "When It's Round-Up Time Up Yonder."

By now, people in town had heard that the famous gospel singer Minnie Oatman was in the cafe, and the place was filling up fast. Opal Butts and several ladies still in pin curlers and hair-nets were the first to arrive from the beauty shop next door.

After Chester finished his song, they all applauded. Then

someone standing in the back of the cafe called out, "Minnie, could you please sing just one song for us?"

Minnie looked around and noticed she had drawn a crowd and said, "Sure, hon." Then she began to play and sing at the top of her lungs her now famous rendition of "Can't Wait to Get to Heaven." Afterward, people lined up to get her autograph. Her husband, Ferris Oatman, finally came to the door and called to her, "Minnie, come on now, hon. We got to be in Pine Mountain by five."

After the Oatmans left town, Buddy Jr. was still awestruck and a little confused by the whole experience. He said, "Aunt Idgie . . . was Chester a real boy?"

"Why, sure he was. He looked right at you, didn't he? And talked."

"Yes, but he was so little. Why was he so little?"

"Well, Buddy, that's the thing, everybody's different. Some people have one arm, some have two. Some are fat, some are skinny, some are little . . . and some people, like myself, are smart." Idgie looked over at Ruth and said, "And then some people I know aren't all that smart."

Ruth picked up a biscuit and threw it at her. Idgie dodged it and laughed. Ruth waited until Idgie had turned her back and threw another one that bounced off the back of Idgie's head. Idgie looked back at her, holding her head. "Hey!"

Ruth smiled and feigned ignorance. "What?" she said.

"You hit me with that biscuit."

Ruth winked at Buddy. "What biscuit? I didn't see any biscuit."

Idgie said, "Buddy, you saw that."

Buddy said, "No ma'am. I didn't see anything."

Idgie then stuck her tongue out at them both and went into the kitchen.

. . .

LATER THAT NIGHT, when Ruth was tucking him in bed, Buddy said, "Momma, I sure did like Chester. Do you think he liked me?"

"Oh, I'm sure he did, sweetheart. He signed a picture for you, didn't he?"

"Hey, Momma, do you think Chester might write to me sometime, like a pen pal?"

While Buddy was sleeping, little Chester had been put back into his suitcase, headed out of Georgia to another town, never knowing what a hit he'd been with Buddy, or that every once in a while, Buddy would be getting a postcard sent from one of the many places they traveled, saying "Hello, Buddy," and signed, "Your friend, Chester."

....

The Weems Weekly

(WHISTLE STOP, ALABAMA'S WEEKLY BULLETIN)
August 17, 1937

OUR SURPRISE VISITOR

I'm sure we are all still not quite over our town being visited by some famous folks. And, looking back, not to brag, but yours truly might have been to blame.

Last week, Wilbur and I went over to Gate City to hear the Oatman Family Gospel Singers. And oh, what a show they put on! I have never seen or heard anything like it. As *Gospel* magazine says, "Pound for pound you will never hear or see a better group than the Ferris and Minnie Oatman Family Singers." Anyhow, we waited in line to get a signed album, and while Minnie was signing mine, I happened to mention that while she was in the area, she needed to come to the Whistle Stop Cafe and have some of Sipsey's famous fried green tomatoes. I could tell she seemed to appreciate good food. And happily for us she did!

Reverend Scroggins was very happy with all the money we took in at the church rummage sale on Saturday. At last count it was over eighty-two dollars. The sale took place in my neighbor Ninny Threadgoode's front yard, and consisted of collectibles, homemade quilts, and pies and cakes all donated by the neighborhood ladies. My other half Wilbur showed up to help and, as usual, fell asleep sitting up in his chair. Opal Butts went over and stuck a "Make an Offer" sign in front of him, and sad to say, we only got one offer from a widow lady from Gate City for five dollars and Opal took it. I had to pay it to get him back! Oh well, it's all for a good cause.

Also, overheard at the cafe the other day: "There are two surefire ways to avoid paying alimony. Don't get married. But if you do, stay married!"

. . . Dot Weems . . .

Amtrak Train

THE GIFT

As Bud and Billy continued talking, Billy said, "Sir, if you don't mind my asking, did you ever feel sorry for yourself? Losing your arm so young like that?"

Bud smiled. "Oh, you bet. For a while I had a bad case of the 'Poor me's' and 'My life is ruined forever, I'll never amount to anything, what's the point of trying.' I was well on my way to becoming a royal jerk. But you know, all that changed. And I can tell you exactly when it happened."

"Did you get an artificial arm or something?"

"Nope, better than that. It started on one Christmas and ended on another, and I remember it just like it happened yesterday." Then he smiled. "That second Christmas, everybody in town knew what I was getting. Everybody but me. But I knew something was up. My friend Naughty Bird was taunting me. She'd say, 'I know what Santa Claus is bringing you,' and then she'd run away. Or else somebody would say, 'I know something that you don't.' I tried my best to find out, but nobody would talk, and I was so darned frustrated, because I knew what I wanted. I wanted it so bad I was scared to tell anybody. Scared I wouldn't get it, scared to let Momma and Aunt Idgie know that I'd be disappointed if I didn't get it.

"Back then I still kind of believed in Santa Claus, so I wrote him a letter addressed to the North Pole, and handed it to Mrs. Weems, the postmistress, in person to make sure it got mailed in time." Bud smiled. "Of course, I didn't know it then, but I found out later that Mrs. Weems read all those letters to 'Santa Claus' herself, and told the parents what their kids wanted. So Momma and Aunt Idgie knew all along what I was hoping for."

A Christmas Tradition

THE FIRST YEAR Idgie and Ruth had opened the cafe, as a thank-you to their customers, they'd decided to stay open Christmas Day and invite everybody in for a free meal.

That first Christmas morning, when Ruth opened the door, she was stunned to see how many people were waiting outside. Almost everybody in town was standing there, including a few strangers who had heard that the cafe would be open. But all were welcome. Men, women, children, folks riding the rails, even dogs and cats.

Every year after that, they started cooking around December twenty-third. They had to. Christmas at the cafe was now a town tradition. And during the Depression, for the poorer kids, the gifts that Ruth and Idgie wrapped and put under the Christmas tree were the only ones they would receive that year. Then there was the food. Sipsey's son, Big George, would make sure there was plenty of barbecue on hand. And a few days before Christmas, Idgie's hunting pals always brought in a load of wild turkeys to fix and stuff with cranberries. They had fried chicken and pork chops, plenty of mashed potatoes and gravy, chicken and dumplings, homemade rolls, cornbread, and biscuits, and at least ten different kinds of dessert. A lot of the railroad men that lived in town were old bachelors, and had nowhere to go on Christmas. The cafe was home to them, and they brought Idgie bottles of good seventy-five-year-old Kentucky bourbon that she served in paper cups to try to fool Reverend Scroggins. Of course, she never did fool him, particularly when a few of the guys got so loaded they fell off their stools.

Just like always, in 1937 everybody in town was enjoying themselves. Everybody except Buddy. A young boy suddenly losing his arm was bad enough. But Buddy had been very good at sports, and had dreamed of becoming a major league baseball pitcher, or a football star. He didn't say much about it, but he hardly ever went outside to play anymore. He just stayed in his room, and for the first time in his life, he'd started throwing little temper fits. That Christmas, after he'd thrown a fit in front of his Aunt Ninny and Uncle Cleo, Idgie knew that Buddy was more upset than even he realized.

Idgie had a friend named Eva Bates who ran the juke joint with her daddy down on the Warrior River. And Idgie had a hunch about something. Eva had about ten dogs that she kept out in her yard. And there was one little dog in particular that Idgie thought might be good for Buddy to see. The problem was that Idgie had made a promise to Ruth, so she was taking a big chance that might be worth taking, but only if he promised her to keep his mouth shut about it. After they got in the car she said, "Now, Buddy, if I take you somewhere today you can't tell anybody because—"

"I know, because you could get in a lot of trouble if I do, right?"

"That's right. So, you promise?"

"I promise."

"Scout's honor?"

"Yes ma'am."

"Okay then." Idgie started the car, and they headed down toward the river.

They drove up to the wooden house and parked, and Idgie left Buddy in the car while she went up on the porch and talked with a lady with bright orange hair. As he sat there for a while, Buddy suddenly noticed the little three-legged dog jumping and running around in the yard with the others. And just as Idgie had hoped, it made an impression. The little dog didn't seem to know she had a leg missing. She just seemed happy to be alive. There was nothing handicapped about her. He got out and called her over to the fence, leaned down, and petted her, and she almost licked his hand off.

When Idgie got back in the car, Buddy said, "Aunt Idgie, I sure do like that little brown dog over there. It's got a leg missing, but it's still cute. Don't you think?"

Idgie looked over at it and said, "I do, and as a matter of fact, I think it's the cutest one in the bunch." She waved to Eva and they drove off.

EVA BATES WAS a somewhat notorious character in the area, as was her father, Big Jack Bates, who owned the Wagon Wheel Fishing Lodge and River Club. The tourist cabins behind the club were known far and wide for "unseemly activity," so to speak. Big Jack Bates, a part-time bootlegger, also ran illegal gambling in the back room of the River Club, where high-stakes poker games could sometimes become dangerous. It was rumored that a couple of men had been murdered back there: one for cheating, the other for reneging on a bet. It was not a safe place, by any means, but Idgie had been going there with her brother since she was eight, and had been playing poker in the back room since she was twelve. And she was good at it.

After Ruth had left Whistle Stop that summer to go home to Valdosta and get married, nobody could control Idgie anymore.

She wound up spending most of her time down at the River Club with Eva and Jack. Idgie didn't care that most so-called decent people in Whistle Stop looked down on them, or that Reverend Scroggins preached against the evils of the River Club, "that dangerous den of iniquity that is corrupting our youth." Eva and Big Jack were Idgie's friends. She liked them, and they liked her.

But later, Ruth left her husband and returned to live in Whistle Stop. It was then, when she and Idgie and little Buddy moved into the back of the cafe, that things changed. For the first three years, Idgie would sneak out at night and go to the River Club to drink and gamble, and Ruth would lie awake all night worrying about her. Finally, Idgie came home drunk one too many times. The last time was when she rolled in at five in the morning with a bloody nose. She'd gotten into a fight with someone at the poker table. The next day, Ruth took little Buddy and moved out.

She said to Idgie, "I love you. But I can't live like this, wondering if you are dead or alive, or if someone has shot you."

Ruth didn't come back, either, until Idgie promised her on the Bible that she would never go down to the River Club again.

A Year Later

BUDDY JUNIOR WAS hunched over the table, looking very serious and determined as he carefully composed his letter.

Dear Santa Claus,

My name is Buddy Threadgoode, Jr., and I live in the back of the Whistle Stop Cafe in Whistle Stop, Alabama. I am eight years old and I have been a very good boy. Ask my mother if you want to. Her name is Ruth. I only want one present this year. I'm not sure if you are real, but I want a dog so much. Momma says it is not good to have a dog where you serve food, but Aunt Idgie said, why not, because we have other animals, too. So please, please, please, bring me a dog. I promise to take very good care of her and love her forever.

Your friend,
Buddy Threadgoode, Jr.

Whistle Stop, Alabama

DECEMBER 25, 1938

THE CHRISTMAS PARTY at the cafe was almost over. Everybody had eaten all they could hold and was happily stuffed with good food, and all the presents had been opened. Santa Claus had already left to go back to the North Pole, and Buddy was trying not to cry. Peggy Hadley had received her doll, Jessie Ray Scroggins had a new BB gun, and Buddy had received a lot of new underwear and a red cowboy hat, but he had not gotten the only thing he'd really wanted.

Later, after all the Christmas carols had been sung, Dot Weems closed up the old piano. But nobody seemed to be leaving to go home.

Idgie, who had been missing from the party for a while, walked back in from the cafe kitchen, looked around, and said, "Hey, Buddy, guess what? Santa just came back and left a present he said he forgot to give you. Should I go get it?"

Buddy looked up. "Yes, ma'am."

Buddy didn't know it, but all eyes were on him. They all knew what was coming.

Idgie came back in carrying a large white box. She put it down and took the top off, and the little three-legged dog jumped out, so happy to be out of the box, she ran around in circles, then she ran right across the room straight to Buddy and started jumping up and down and licking his face.

Buddy was clearly beside himself with joy and blurted out, "Look, Aunt Idgie, it's the same one we saw at down at the River Club. And she remembered me!"

Ruth quickly turned and looked at Idgie, but Idgie pretended she didn't see her.

Later that night, after everyone had gone home, Ruth said, "Idgie, I thought you told everyone you found that dog."

"I did find it."

"Did you find it in Eva Bates's yard?"

"I may have. I don't remember."

Ruth knew Idgie well. When she didn't remember something it was a sure sign that she had done it.

In the past, Ruth and Idgie had a problem where Eva Bates was concerned. And under any other circumstances, Ruth would have been very upset to know that Idgie had taken Buddy anywhere around the River Club. But when she saw that Buddy was so happy with his new puppy, she couldn't be mad. Not tonight.

THE NEXT MORNING, a hungover Eva Bates picked up the phone at the River Club.

"Mrs. Bates, this is Ruth Jamison calling, Buddy's mother."

"Oh . . . um . . . yeah?"

"I was calling to thank you. That was a very sweet thing you did, giving him that little dog. He just adores it."

Eva was delighted to speak with her. She had never met Ruth, but she knew all about her.

She replied cheerfully, "Oh that's no never mind, Ms. Jamison. I got me lots of 'em. I could tell when he first seed that little threeleggedy thing in the yard, he tooked to it right off from the start. So after the boy left that day, red flags started to shoot out every which a way, and it hit me. Both of 'em had a limb that was goned. So I tole Idgie she could have it for the boy, if she wanted it."

AFTER RUTH SAID goodbye, she had a change of mind about Eva. Unsavory reputation or not, the woman clearly had a heart of gold.

The Weems Weekly

(WHISTLE STOP, ALABAMA'S WEEKLY BULLETIN)
December 28, 1938

A JOLLY TIME

ANOTHER YEAR IS almost over, and what a year it has been. Sipsey and Big George really outdid themselves Christmas Day. How so much good food can come out of that little kitchen is just beyond me, and it just kept coming all day long. I counted at least twenty-three turkeys and a lot more pies and cakes. Idgie and Ruth spoil us all. And I'm sure we all agree, Christmas just wouldn't be Christmas if we didn't spend it at the cafe. I don't know how those gals manage to wrap that many presents, and decorate so beautifully.

I especially loved all the shiny red Christmas balls Idgie hung on the deer head above the counter!

Anyhow, thanks for the good vittles and the good time year after year. And of course Christmas really wouldn't be Christmas without our annual visit from Santa.

With Christmas over, New Year's Resolutions time is almost here again. Last night I started my list, and to my surprise they are the same old ones I make every year and never keep. Oh well, better luck next year. The only one I do keep is to always be grateful for what we have. And as Reverend Scroggins said last Sunday, "A grateful heart is a happy heart," and, boy, am I grateful that we are living in this wonderful free country of ours. I read the news and it saddens me that so many people around the world are suffering.

On a happier note, I never saw a happier child than Buddy Threadgoode, Jr. It's so good to see him smile again. The little dog he got for Christmas seems to have made all the difference to a sweet boy who deserves it.

Also, Wilbur dropped a bowling ball on his foot and broke two toes, in case you were wondering why he is limping.

. . . Dot Weems . . .

P.S. I THINK we might have some snow tomorrow. Another holiday miracle is afoot. So be on the lookout.

Whistle Stop, Alabama

DECEMBER 29, 1938

Dear Santa Claus,

I am writing to thank you for my dog, Lady. I am sorry I didn't think you were real, but you are, and I love you so much for bringing her to me. She was the very dog I wanted. I don't mind that she has a leg missing at all. I have an arm missing, and I used to mind but now I don't. Lady does not feel sorry for herself one bit and neither do I anymore. We have fun and she can jump up and catch a stick. I can throw a ball, too.

I don't need anything next year. Thanks again.

Your friend forever,
Buddy Threadgoode, Jr.

P.S. Let me know if I can ever do anything for you.

Amtrak Train

"So there I was, Christmas almost over, and I didn't get what I wanted, so of course I decided then and there that I didn't believe in Santa Claus. Then at the last minute Aunt Idgie brings in the very dog I wanted. You know, Billy, life can be hard sometimes. And I sort of think animals are little gifts the good Lord sends to help us get through it. Lady sure did that for me."

"What kind of a dog was she?"

"I don't know. I guess she was some kind of terrier mix. Just a good old mutt. But she came out of that box and I was never so happy in all my life, except maybe the day my daughter Ruthie was born. Oh, how I loved that dog. She slept with me, ate with me, never left my side for a moment. She was my pal. And whenever I'd get upset over something, she knew it. She would run around barking, acting silly, just to make me laugh. You couldn't be sad around her if you tried. Always happy to see me. Poor old thing, she stayed with me as long as she could. But even on the day she died, she was still wagging her tail, still happy to see me. I tell you, when I buried her it just about killed me. I don't think I'll ever get over it, but that's okay. Small price to pay for what she gave me. And that's what you get when you love something that much. Joy and heartbreak."

Billy sighed. "I know what you mean about love being a joy and a heartbreak. My fiancée just broke up with me."

"No. A handsome guy like you? Why?"

Billy looked down. "She felt oppressed."

"What did you do to her?"

"I asked her to quit her job."

"Oh, I see. What does she do?"

"She's a fire-person."

"A what?"

"A fireman, only she's a fire-person. I think her job's far too dangerous, but she doesn't. So we broke up . . . well . . . she broke up."

"Oh. Well, that's a hard one. I see your point . . . but on the other hand my daughter Ruthie gave up on having a career when she got married, and now she regrets it."

"Does she?"

"Yes, she does. You know, your fiancée doing dangerous work may be hard on the marriage in the short run, but if putting out fires makes her happy, and you love her . . ."

"Oh, I do," he said sadly.

"Well . . . it might be best to just go along with it."

"Think so?"

"I do. You want a happy wife. And I'll tell you something else. I'd sure like to meet her. I never met a lady fireman."

Billy's eyes lit up with pride. "She's very strong. She can pick me up."

"No foolin'," said Bud.

"Yes sir. She can pick me up and run a hundred yards with me slung over her shoulder."

"Yeah?"

"Yeah."

"Well, Billy, you never know. Someday that just might come in handy."

Going Home

As THE TRAIN got closer to Birmingham, Bud started to get excited. He said to Billy, "Could I ask a big favor? Would you switch seats with me? I sure would like to look out the window and try to see Whistle Stop."

"Oh, of course, no problem."

Bud sat by the window and looked out when they passed by where he thought it should be, but he never did see the Whistle Stop crossing sign, and he was disappointed. Oh well, maybe he would see it on the way back to Atlanta this afternoon.

When THEY PULLED into Birmingham, Bud saw that they had torn down the beautiful old Birmingham terminal station, with the seventy-five-foot glass ceiling. The train stopped at a small, nondescript Amtrak station somewhere downtown.

They stepped off the train, and Billy walked with Bud to the small waiting room. "I sure enjoyed talking to you, Mr. Threadgoode."

"Same here, Billy, and good luck with your studies and your girlfriend."

"Thank you, and thanks for the advice. I just texted her and hopefully she'll answer."

After he said goodbye to Billy, Bud sat down to wait. He looked at his watch and realized he had an hour before his train back to

Atlanta departed. He might be able to do it, if he hurried. He quickly stepped outside the station and onto the street. Luckily there was a cab letting someone out, and he was able to flag it down.

Bud got in the cab, saw the driver's name, and said, "Hi, Pete."

"Hello there. Where can I take you today?"

"Well, that's just it. I don't have an exact address. It's a little town called Whistle Stop."

The driver punched up the map on his GPS and looked. . . . "I don't see it here."

"Look near Gate City. You should see Whistle Stop close by."

"No, it's not on the map."

"No? Huh. Well, I do know it's twelve minutes east of Birmingham, but with all the new interstates and superhighways they built, I'm not sure where I am anymore. The easiest way is to follow the railroad tracks east. I'll recognize the road when we get there. There's just one way in and out."

As they drove through downtown, Buddy looked out the window. "Boy, this place sure has changed. My Aunt Idgie used to bring us over here to the movie theaters when I was a kid, but I don't see any of them now."

"Naw, they tore most of those down a long time ago."

As they drove for a while following the railroad tracks, the driver said, "Does anything look familiar?"

"No . . . not yet. But it's somewhere around here." The driver went a little farther, and about fifteen minutes later, he said, "Should I just keep driving?"

"I'll tell you what, Pete, why don't you park and let me walk ahead a little and see if I can figure out where I am. You can leave your meter on, and if I don't see anything familiar in the next five minutes I'll come on back."

Pete could see the old man was upset, and he felt sorry for him. He turned his meter off. He would give him some time.

Bud got out and started walking along the tracks. He had ridden the train to Atlanta and back hundreds of times, but today he was having a hard time recognizing anything. He passed a few falling-down brick buildings, but they didn't look familiar. As he walked a little farther, he looked down and saw an old wooden sign lying on the ground down below the tracks. He wondered if it was from someplace he knew, something that could help him get his bearings. So he walked down the embankment and turned it over. The sign just said GROCERIES, but no location. He looked around and spotted another old part of the sign about twenty feet away. He went down and kicked it over, but it was blank. He looked for another part of the sign that might have the location written on it, but no luck. He had gone so far down into the woods, he almost didn't find his way back to the tracks. And when he did, he was all turned around. He couldn't figure out which direction he had come from, and then realized he was completely lost. All he needed was to fall and break a hip out here in the middle of nowhere. Then God knows what would happen. If he just had his phone he could call somebody. Now there was nothing to do but head back in the direction he thought he had come from and hope to hell he was right.

Pete the cab driver figured the old man must have found the place he was looking for. The guy'd said to give him five minutes, and he had already waited forty-five and he hadn't come back yet. He hated to do it but he had no choice, so he started up the car and headed back toward Birmingham.

ALMOST AN HOUR later, Bud was still walking. He had seen nothing but a bunch of woods on either side. He looked at his watch.

Oh Lordy . . . now he was in trouble. He had missed his train back to Atlanta. After a while, he just stopped walking and stood in the middle of the tracks and called out as loudly as he could: "Hey! Hey! I need some help!" He waited, but nobody answered. He stood there for quite some time. Then Bud realized he needed to get off the tracks before it got dark, or he could really get hurt. He looked around. He could make out a few trees down below the tracks on his right, and while there was still enough light, he carefully made his way toward the trees, but the embankment was so steep that he slipped and skidded on his backside all the way down. He got up and brushed himself off, then picked out a big tree in a clearing and sat down on the leaves underneath it.

He was stuck here. All he could do was wait until morning and hope that nobody at Briarwood missed him who would then call Ruthie.

"Well, this is a fine mess I've gotten myself into. What in the hell was I thinking? This is terrible. I can't even find my hometown."

As THE NIGHT progressed, Bud was thankful it was not pitch-dark. The moon had come up and was pretty bright, but it was getting cold. He could still see his watch if he held it a certain way. Oh, brother. It was only 9:14. He still had a long night ahead of him. Just then an owl up above hooted.

All Over the News

AFTER THE CONVERSATION with Mr. Merris, Ruthie had called the police and spoken to someone in the missing persons department, who assured her they were checking all the hospitals and that as soon as her father was located or they had any information at all, they would call her immediately.

Ruthie spent the rest of the night pacing back and forth, waiting for any news. Not knowing where he could possibly have gone was causing her imagination to run away with her. Had he been hit by a car? Had he been mugged and shot, and was he lying somewhere bleeding? As more time went by with no word, she imagined a hundred different scenarios.

By six A.M. the next morning, when he had not returned, the police issued an all-points missing person's alert and a photograph of Mr. Threadgoode popped up on the Atlanta Alert Network.

Strangely enough, it was waitress Jasmine Squibb who worked at the Waffle House who called in first. She reported that she had waited on the man in the photo yesterday morning, and that he had told her he was headed for a train trip to Birmingham and back. She then added that he had ordered ham and two eggs over easy with bacon, and was a very good tipper.

As soon as that info came in, the Birmingham authorities were alerted and his photo was posted on Ala.news.com and on the local station WBRC-TV, with the caption, "At-risk senior James Buddy Threadgoode, Jr., is missing from his home in Atlanta, thought to have boarded a train to Birmingham. May or may not have one arm. Anyone with any information, please contact the Birmingham Police Department."

Luckily, Pete the cab driver saw the alert go across his TV screen in Birmingham and called the police. "I picked that man up at the train station yesterday, and dropped him off at the railroad tracks, way out past the old Montgomery Highway. He was looking for someplace called Whistle Stop, and the last time I saw him he was walking down the tracks, headed east. I waited as long as I could, but he never came back, so I figured he must have found the place he was looking for. Poor old guy. I feel terrible about leaving him."

Within minutes, a team of first responders headed for the railroad tracks and started walking in both directions, with a megaphone calling out "Mr. Threadgoode! Mr. Buddy Threadgoode!"

After about thirty minutes, they heard someone yelling, "Hey, hey . . . here I am. Down here."

They looked down the embankment and saw an old man sitting under a tree waving one arm at them. He had taken off his other arm to sleep.

As the paramedics approached him, he said, "I'm awful glad to see you guys. I'm about frozen to death." Bud tried to stand up but he was so stiff, he needed help to pull him to his feet. And before he knew it he was up the hill and in the back of an ambulance, wrapped in a blanket and headed to the hospital.

When a dispatcher at the police department heard that the old man they found by the railroad tracks had been trying to go home to Whistle Stop, he told his wife, "I'm glad he didn't find it."

"Why?"

"Because there's nothing out there anymore but junk and weeds."

Get Me to Birmingham

ATLANTA, GEORGIA

AT 9:08 THAT morning, when the phone finally rang, Ruthie was so distraught that she almost fainted.

It was a man's voice, calling from the police department. "Mrs. Caldwell, good news. We found your father, and he's alive."

"Oh, thank God. Where was he?"

"He was . . . uh . . . let me read the report, we just got it in. Oh. It says he was found by the railroad tracks."

"What railroad tracks?"

"It doesn't say. Just somewhere outside Birmingham, Alabama."

Ruthie was stunned. "Birmingham? What was he doing in Birmingham?"

"I couldn't say. You'll have to ask him. All I have is the report. Right now he's at the UAB Hospital in Birmingham."

"Oh no. Is he hurt?"

"I don't think so, ma'am. It just says he's being held under observation."

"Oh . . . thank you. Thank you so much."

"You're welcome, ma'am. Glad to be of service."

Ruthie didn't have time to waste; she had to get to her father right away. She booked herself on the next flight to Birmingham at 10:55. She threw a little makeup on, grabbed her purse, and ran to her car.

As she was frantically driving across town to the airport, she knowingly broke the law, looking up a number while driving, but she had to know.

"UAB Hospital. How may I direct you your call?"

"I'm not sure. My father, Mr. James Bud Threadgoode, is a patient in your hospital, and I need to know his condition. I'm his daughter, and I'm in traffic in Atlanta."

"One moment please."

Then a dial tone.

"Oh God. Disconnected." Ruthie pulled her phone out of her purse, looking for the redial button.

Just then, a man in the car next to her wagged his finger at her for being on the phone and then gave her the finger. Not being her usual polite self, she gave it right back and yelled, "My father is in the hospital in Alabama, you asshole."

He sped up and drove off.

Then she heard a voice say, "UAB Hospital. How may I direct your call?"

She didn't know, so she guessed, "The People Under Observation Ward, please."

After a moment, someone picked up. "Nurse's station, Terry speaking."

"Oh, hi, Terry. . . . Thank heavens. I'm calling about Bud Threadgoode. I'm his daughter, Ruthie Caldwell. Could you tell me his condition, please? I'm in Atlanta and I'm trying to get there as soon as I can."

"Hold on, honey."

The nurse came back on the phone. "I just checked Mr. Threadgoode's chart, and his condition appears to be stable."

"Oh, thank you. Please tell him I'm on my way and I'll get there as fast as I can."

"Take your time, sweetie. Trust me, he's not going anywhere."

As Ruthie was parking her car at the airport, the word "stable" kept running around in her mind. "Stable . . . that sounds good. She didn't say 'critical,' she said 'stable.'" So she calmed down a little and was grateful she could see her terminal up ahead.

BACK IN BIRMINGHAM, Terry, the roly-poly friendly nurse, walked into Bud's room and said, "Your daughter just called and said she's on her way over from Atlanta."

"How does she know I'm here?" Bud asked.

"Honey, you've been all over the news."

Bud, who was hooked up to an IV drip for dehydration, nodded. "Oh . . . did she sound mad?"

"No. She sounded worried, though, and I don't blame her." She went over and checked his drip, then smiled at him. "You old scalawag, running away like that. You're lucky they found you when they did, still all in one piece." Then she looked at him. "Well, almost."

ONCE THE PLANE took off for the short thirty-five-minute flight to Birmingham, and the seat belt sign went off, Ruthie finally went to the ladies' room. She was horrified when she saw herself in the mirror. In her haste to get to the airport, she had tried to throw on a little makeup, but somehow she had only made up one eye. No wonder people had been looking at her strangely.

Bud in Birmingham

WHEN BUD SAW Ruthie walking into his hospital room, the first thing he said was, "Oops. I sorta messed up, didn't I? I'm sorry, honey."

"Daddy, are you all right? I've been worried to death about you."

"I'm fine, just a little embarrassed I got lost. I didn't mean to cause all this trouble."

"Are you sure you're not hurt anywhere?"

"Nope, just a few scrapes, and I pulled something in my back when I skidded down a hill."

"You look very pale. Are you sure you're feeling all right?"

"I'm sure."

He had always been her big, tall, handsome daddy. But today, for the first time, she couldn't help but notice how much he had aged, and just how small he looked lying in that bed.

"What in the world were you doing coming all the way over to Birmingham by yourself, and walking on the railroad tracks in the freezing cold?"

"Well, I was trying to find Whistle Stop. I thought I knew where it was, but evidently I was wrong."

"Thank God they found you. Did you know you had people in two states looking for you? Your picture was all over the TV and everything."

"I'm sorry, Ruthie. I knew you'd be mad."

"I'm not mad. I'm just . . . why didn't you call me and tell me where you were?"

"I would have, but I forgot my phone."

Ruthie sighed and shook her head. "You crazy old man. What am I going to do with you?"

"I don't know. But now . . . there's something else."

"Oh Lord. What?"

"You'd better sit down."

Ruthie sat in the chair by the bed and waited.

"Promise me you won't get upset."

"I promise . . . what else?"

"I lost my arm."

"What? How did you do that?"

"I was trying to sleep and it was bothering me. So I took it off. Then when those EMT guys showed up, I was so glad to see them that I forgot to pick it up."

"Oh, Daddy."

"Now, I might be able to find it, if I could just figure out where I was. I could go back and try to look for it."

"Absolutely not. You are not going to go wandering around in any more woods. Just forget it. Your arm can be replaced, but you can't. Do you realize you could have caught pneumonia, or fallen and hit your head? What were you thinking?"

"Well . . . at the time, I was thinking I hope somebody finds me."

Then Bud looked at her and noticed something strange. "What's the matter with your eye?"

"Nothing. And why did you just take off like that, and not let anybody know where you were going?"

"I was trying to not cause anybody any trouble. I thought I wouldn't be missed. But that didn't work out."

"No, it didn't. The good news is the doctor says that other than the effects of hypothermia and a little dehydration, you seem to be okay."

"Good. When are they going to spring me out of here?"

"Terry just told me they need to keep you a couple of days, just to make sure your blood pressure remains stable and your electrolytes are good."

"Oh darn. I'm so sorry, honey. Here I was trying not to bother you and now look at what a mess I've caused."

"That's all right, Daddy. Just as long as you're okay and not dead in a ditch somewhere."

She gently pushed his hair off his forehead and took his hand.

"You know you're the only daddy I have. I love you. And I need you to stay around as long as you can."

"I'll try my best, honey."

She smiled. "So from now on you are grounded young man, okay? No more crazy trips, all right?"

He nodded and held up two fingers. "Scout's honor."

The entire time she had been talking to her father, the cellphone in her purse had been ringing. Finally she took it out and looked. It was her daughter, Carolyn, calling from Washington.

"I'm sorry, Daddy, I need to take this." She stepped out into the hall and picked up. She was hoping Carolyn was just calling to say hello, but no such luck. She was frantic.

"Mother! Where are you? Grandmother called and said that Granddaddy has gone insane and ran away from Briarwood, and spent all night under some tree in Birmingham. Is that right?"

"No, honey, he's not insane. He just took a little trip and got lost, that's all."

"And where are you? She said you just picked up and left without telling her a thing."

"Carolyn, just calm down. I'm at the hospital in Birmingham with Granddaddy."

"Hospital! Why is he in the hospital?"

"He's just a little dehydrated, so they're keeping him under observation for a couple of days."

"Oh. Well, do you need me to come down there? I could fly out in the morning, I guess, but I'd have to come right back. We're giving a dinner party for twelve people, including Brian's boss and his wife, so I can't just cancel it at the last minute."

"No, no, honey. You don't need to come. We'll only be here a short while. You take care of your party and I'll call you when we get home. Okay?"

"Well . . . if you say so. I'm glad he's all right, but really, Mother, what's wrong with him? Running away from Briarwood and embarrassing Grandmother like that? She said it's been in the papers and everything. And after all the trouble she went to getting him in there in the first place."

"Honey, I have to go. I'll tell Granddaddy you said hello."

RUTHIE WENT BACK in his room and smiled. "That was Carolyn, wanting to know how you were. She sends her love and hopes you feel better soon."

"Did you tell her where I was?"

"No, that was the lovely Martha Lee, who just couldn't wait to call her and tell her that you had spent the night under a tree."

"Oh darn. I was hoping she wouldn't find out."

Just then, Nurse Terry walked in the room and Bud said, "Hey, Terry, this is my daughter, Ruthie."

Terry nodded. "I know. We met over the phone, and now that she's here, I hope you'll behave yourself. Did you tell your daughter that you told me you were John D. Rockefeller?"

"Oh, Daddy. You didn't."

"I thought I might get better treatment, but she poked holes in me anyway. The woman is a vampire. Look out, Ruthie, or she'll start going after you next."

Her father was clearly going to be okay. She could tell he already had the nurses eating out of his hand.

LATER THAT DAY, Ruthie called a cab to take her to a nearby hotel. She was exhausted and desperately needed a nice, warm bath and a nap. In her rush to get to Birmingham she hadn't packed a thing. All she had with her were her purse and the clothes she was wearing. After she checked in, she stopped at a little convenience shop in the hotel lobby and picked up a toothbrush and some toothpaste. She would worry about the rest later.

Bud was glad Ruthie had been so sweet about him losing his arm. She had gone to so much trouble to make sure he had the best prosthesis they could buy. He wished he could go back and try to find the damn thing but he knew, even if she would let him go back and look for it, the chances of him finding the exact tree where he'd left it were one in a million.

Bud didn't know it, but he had been to that very tree once before. It hadn't been as tall then, but neither had he. He had only been six years old when his Aunt Idgie had taken him to her secret bee tree. And there was more to the bee tree than he knew.

A Kindred Spirit

BIRMINGHAM, ALABAMA

EVELYN COUCH AND her husband, Ed, were, as they say, "sitting pretty." They owned a lovely home, four nice cars, and a large luxury motor home. But after Ed passed away in 2011, Evelyn sold her car dealerships and retired. Now she mostly played bridge and managed her portfolio of property investments she had made over the years. But she was bored.

That morning, Evelyn had been sitting at her breakfast table drinking coffee and watching the local news, when a Missing Person Alert ran across the bottom of the screen.

The missing senior, Mr. James Buddy Threadgoode, eighty-four, was last seen in Atlanta, and thought to be headed to Birmingham. White male, five foot eleven inches tall, blue eyes, white hair, believed to be missing left arm, and last seen wearing a plaid wool jacket.

When Evelyn first saw the name, it caught her attention, but then when she read the description, she knew it had to be him. How many people with one arm named Buddy Threadgoode in their eighties could there be? He just had to be Ruth and Idgie's little boy. The one she had heard so much about from her friend Ninny Threadgoode.

She suddenly became very excited and called Harry, her friend in the newsroom at the local TV station, and asked the status of the missing man and was told he had not been located as of yet. Before she hung up, she asked him to please call and let her know if they find him. Oh, she hoped he would be found. She would just love to somehow get in touch with him.

She didn't know Bud, but she felt as if she did. Ninny Threadgoode had told her so much about Whistle Stop and the cafe, and Evelyn remembered that Buddy had married his childhood sweetheart and that they had a daughter. She also knew that they had moved, but she didn't know to where. But if she could find him, she had something she had always wanted to give him—something she thought his daughter might certainly love to have. She had kept it for years. When Ninny passed away, she'd left Evelyn a shoebox of old photos of the cafe, some of the old menus and cafe recipes, and many photographs of Idgie, Ruth, and Buddy Jr. that really should be given back to the Threadgoode family.

AROUND TWO O'CLOCK, her friend Harry from the television station called and told her that Mr. Threadgoode had been found alive and well, and that he was at UAB Hospital under observation.

Evelyn was thrilled and called the hospital right away. Terry, who was still on duty, had answered "Observation, this is Terry."

"Hey, Terry, this is Evelyn Couch, and I was wondering if I could possibly get some information about Bud Threadgoode?"

Terry said, "Is this *the* Evelyn Couch, who did all those Cadillac commercials on TV?"

"Yes."

"Oh, for heaven's sake. I used to see you on TV all the time. How are you?"

"Just fine, thank you, Terry. Listen, hon, I don't want to bother him, but I'm trying to get in touch with Mr. Threadgoode's daughter and—"

"You just missed her. She just left."

"She's in Birmingham?"

"Yes. Flew in today. I have her name and number, would you like it?"

"Thank you so much, Terry, I owe you one."

"Oh, you're welcome. But she may be trying to take a nap, so I'd wait a little while to call."

"Thanks, I will."

RUTHIE WOKE UP at around four-thirty that afternoon and wondered if she should try to get a cab back to the hospital. But they had her phone number, so she was sure if there had been any changes in Bud's condition they would have called. Now, she didn't know what to do. Here she was sitting all alone in some strange, ugly hotel room, in a town where she didn't know a soul. She looked out the window and saw that it was starting to get dark outside. She decided to go ahead and call the hospital. They told her her father was sleeping, so she turned on the television set as a diversion, and was watching a rerun of *Shark Tank* when the phone rang.

"Mrs. Caldwell, my name is Evelyn Couch. You don't know me, but I was very good friends with someone I believe was your father's aunt."

"Really?"

"Yes. Her name was Ninny Threadgoode."

"That's right. He did have an Aunt Ninny."

"Married to a man named Cleo, and they had a son named Albert?"

"Yes, that's exactly right. He talks about them all the time. Oh, wait until I tell Daddy."

"Oh my goodness. I'm so glad I found you. It's a long story, Mrs. Caldwell, but Ninny Threadgoode was a very special person in my life and I would love to tell him about it sometime. Would that be possible?"

"Of course."

"They told me at the hospital that your father is doing well, and I know you must be relieved. That must have been quite a scare."

"Yes, it was."

"Listen, I know this is a bad time, and I don't want to bother you, but if you and your father ever get back to Birmingham for any reason, would you call me? I have something I think you might like to have."

"We'd love that. Do you ever get to Atlanta?"

"Not much, since it got so big. The last time I was there I was lost for three hours. I mean, how many Peachtree Streets are there? But I'm game to try again."

Ruthie laughed. "It is confusing, I know."

"Anyhow, I'm so glad your father is all right."

"Thank you. The doctor feels pretty sure I'll probably be able to take him back home in a couple of days."

"Are you over here by yourself?"

"Yes."

"Do you have friends in Birmingham?"

"No, not really."

"Well, listen, if there's anything I can do for you, please let me know. I'm not that far away. I can bring you anything you need. What are you going to do for your dinner tonight?"

"I haven't even thought about it. Room service, I guess."

"Oh, don't do that. Let me come pick you up and take you someplace nice for dinner."

"You're so sweet. But, honestly, I look too terrible to go anywhere. I don't have a stitch of makeup with me and my hair is a mess."

Evelyn laughed. "Well, if makeup is your problem, you have no worries. I have makeup, believe me. Anything you need, I've got. Do you have a car?"

"No. I flew over and took a cab to the hospital. I guess I should rent something while I'm here."

"Oh, don't spend your money on that. Let me lend you a car while you're here. I have a few extra cars. Or, better yet, I would be more than happy to take you anywhere you need to go."

"Oh, I can't impose on you."

"Believe me, it's not imposition. I'm a retired person and I am free as a bird and would just love to have something to do and someone to do it with. All my other friends ever want to do is sit around and play bridge."

Ruthie didn't know who this woman was, but whoever she was, God bless her.

The thought of trying to make her way around in a strange town was not very appealing. And she *was* hungry. She'd completely forgotten to have lunch!

ABOUT THIRTY MINUTES later, Ruthie heard someone knocking on her hotel door. When she opened it, there stood a sweet-looking, plump gray-haired lady holding a clear plastic carrying case full of Mary Kay makeup and a huge jar of Mary Kay cold cream. "Hi, Ruthie, I'm Evelyn." Ruthie, who had never laid eyes on this woman before tonight, was so happy to see a friendly face, she wanted to grab her and hug her, right there on the spot.

While she was in the bathroom putting on her new beautiful makeup and they had talked a bit more, Ruthie realized there was something about Evelyn that reminded her of her mother. Maybe it was the accent or her voice—she didn't know what—but it was so comforting to be with someone so clearly down-to-earth, and so real. She had missed that. She had forgotten what it was like to be with someone she could just be herself with.

EVELYN HAD TAKEN them to a lovely four-star restaurant. Ruthie had two glasses of wine with dinner and she certainly wasn't drunk, but she must have been more relaxed than she knew because, by the end of the evening, she had told Evelyn—a complete stranger—all about herself and her life in Atlanta. And Evelyn had been most sympathetic. "I had a mother-in-law from hell myself," she said. "But this Martha Lee character sounds like a real piece of work."

At the end of the evening, Ruthie tried to pay the check, but Evelyn insisted. "No, as long as you are in Birmingham, you are my guest." Besides, she didn't stand a chance. The waiter would not take Ruthie's card.

"Sorry," he said to Ruthie. "What Mrs. Couch wants, Mrs. Couch gets."

"All right, Evelyn," she said, "but when you come to Atlanta, I'm taking you."

EVELYN HADN'T KNOWN what to expect, but she had been taken with Ruthie right away. She had seen a photograph of her grandmother Ruth Jamison, and had been surprised at how much Ruthie looked like her. Very pretty face, same big brown eyes, slender figure. And she was just as nice as she could be.

But after dinner, after getting to know her a little, it was clear to Evelyn that Ruthie could use a friend to talk to. She seemed to be a bit of a lost soul, a little beaten down by something.

Driving back home that night, something else had occurred to Evelyn. Maybe the reason she had felt such an immediate connection with Ruthie was that she had reminded her of her former self. Before she met Ninny.

The Connection

THE NEXT MORNING, Ruthie walked into her father's hospital room, kissed him, and said, "Daddy, I have someone who wants to meet you. You're not going to believe this but she was a very good friend of your Aunt Ninny's."

Bud sat up and looked at the lady with her with surprise and said, "You don't mean it."

Evelyn walked over and shook his hand. "Hey, Mr. Threadgoode. My name is Evelyn Couch. I'm so happy to meet you."

"Same here, Evelyn. Sorry I can't stand up and greet you properly, but I am curious. You look so young. How did you know my Aunt Ninny?"

"It's a long story, but years ago, my husband's mother was in the same nursing home as Ninny was here in Birmingham, and I met her there and we became friends."

"Well I'll be. How nice."

"Yes, it was nice for me, I just adored her. Anyhow, I feel like I know you already. Ninny told me so much about your mother and Idgie Threadgoode, and so many wonderful stories about you."

"Really?"

"Oh yes. She told me all about you growing up in Whistle Stop."

Ruthie jumped in. "Daddy, Evelyn has been so nice. Last

night she took me to the most beautiful restaurant for dinner and she's invited me to stay in her guesthouse."

"That's wonderful. But tell me, how did you two get together?"

Evelyn laughed. "That's the funniest thing, Mr. Threadgoode. Yesterday I was watching television when I saw your name come across the screen as being missing, and I just knew it had to be you, so I called my friend at the television station and asked him to let me know if they found you, because I wanted to get in touch with you."

Ruthie added, "So then she found out that you were here and called, and Terry gave her my number and she called me at the hotel."

"Well . . . isn't it a small world? I sure do appreciate your being so nice to my girl, Evelyn."

"Oh, listen, Mr. Threadgoode, the pleasure is all mine. You have no idea what all your Aunt Ninny did for me. I'm just thrilled to have the chance to say hello to somebody that knew her, too. She just meant the world to me. She was probably the kindest person I ever met."

"Oh, she was that." Then he laughed. "She could also be really funny, but she didn't know it. We used to get the biggest kick out of her. Did she ever tell you she thought the blackbirds sitting on the telephone wire were listening to her phone conversations through their feet?"

Evelyn laughed. "Yes, she did."

"Did she tell you about her son, Albert?"

"Oh, yes."

"Albert was never quite right, but she took care of him every day of his life. I'm just sorry I didn't get to see much of her those last years. We were living up in Maryland when she died."

Evelyn nodded. "I was in California when I heard about it, and by the time I found out, they'd already had the funeral."

"Bless her heart. She was the best old soul."

"Yes she was. But I'll bet she'd be glad to know we got to meet each other after all these years."

Bud said, "Isn't life strange, Ruthie? If I hadn't gotten lost, we would never have met this nice lady."

AFTER PROMISING TO come back to see him tomorrow, Evelyn and Ruthie said goodbye and left Bud to have his lunch and a nap. Bud was so happy. Meeting Evelyn was like suddenly running into an old friend. Somebody who remembered him when.

AS THEY WALKED out of Bud's room, Evelyn turned to Ruthie and said, "Well, if he is not the cutest old man I ever met, I don't know who is. What a doll. Thank you so much for letting me meet him."

"I'm sure the pleasure was all his," Ruthie said. "You just perked him up to no end, talking all about the old days at the cafe. But I have to warn you, get ready. He will talk your ear off about growing up in Whistle Stop." After they stopped at the nurse's station and had a nice little chat with Terry, they headed out.

When they got back in Evelyn's big pink Cadillac, Evelyn said, "Now, the first thing we're going to do is check you out of that hotel, then we're going to do a little shopping and head back home. Because at four P.M., you are booked for a two-hour massage."

Ruthie's eyes lit up. "Two hours?"

"Yes, and then dinner and bed. I figure you could use a little TLC right now, after what all you have been through."

Ruthie sat back in the large soft white leather seat and smiled. "Oh, Evelyn. Where have you been all my life? I'm mere putty in your hands. Lead on."

More Than Meets the Eye

EVELYN'S HOUSE WAS a large rambling white brick home with green shutters that sat right on a beautiful golf course. "Ed played golf," she explained. The guesthouse was a two-bedroom cottage facing a lovely pool. And as if that wasn't impressive enough, it had a huge bathroom with a steam room, a Jacuzzi tub, and a massage room.

Evelyn said, "Now, isn't this better than that hotel room?"

"I should say so."

"You make yourself at home, have a nap or whatever, and Sonia will be here at four for your massage."

Ruthie said, "Evelyn, I can't thank you enough."

Later, Sonia gave her probably the best massage she had ever had in her life, and while she was still lying there on the table, Ruthie said, "You know, Sonia, I noticed Evelyn has a lot of Mary Kay products everywhere. She must really like them."

Sonia said, "Oh, she does. She used to sell them."

"Really?"

"That was before she went into the car business."

"Car business?"

"She didn't tell you? Oh yes, she owned Cadillac dealerships all over Alabama. Did her own commercials and everything."

As Ruthie was finding out, there was a lot more to Evelyn Couch than met the eye.

She had wondered why Terry had wanted Evelyn's autograph.

. . .

THAT NIGHT, EVELYN showed her the picture of Ninny Threadgoode she kept on her desk. Then Evelyn gave her the shoebox
she had inherited from Ninny. Ruthie opened the envelope and
looked at the old photographs inside over and over again. It was so
odd to see how much she looked like her grandmother, Ruth.
One was a photo of her taken when she was around twenty-two
and had first come to Whistle Stop to teach Sunday school for the
summer and was living in the old Threadgoode house. She was
wearing a white dress, standing in the front yard looking up at
somebody who was sitting in a chinaberry tree. All you could see
of the person was two bare feet hanging down. Evelyn said that
Ninny had told her it was Idgie's feet when she'd been about fifteen or sixteen.

Another photo had been taken five years later, after Ruth had
left her husband and had come back to live in Whistle Stop. She
was standing in front of the brand-new cafe, holding a beautiful
baby boy, which Ruthie knew was her father. Idgie, a tall, slender
young woman with short, curly blond hair, was standing behind
her, pointing at the brand-new WHISTLE STOP CAFE sign and smiling. They looked so young to be running a cafe.

She wished she had met her grandmother. There were so
many questions she would have asked her. Why had she left her
husband and moved to Alabama? Her mother had told her there
were absolutely no pictures of Ruth's husband anywhere. Her father didn't seem to know much about him, or care. But still,
Ruthie would have loved to at least have seen a picture of him. He
must have been handsome, because her daddy had always been
such a good-looking man.

The Wonder Boy

December 1940

THERE WAS NO question that Buddy had a curious mind. But then, as Idgie had feared might happen one day, he wondered about something she'd hoped like hell that he wouldn't.

On that particular day, Idgie had taken him over to Loveman's department store in Birmingham to buy him some new shoes, and as they were driving back home, completely of the blue, Buddy turned to her and said, "Aunt Idgie, did you ever know my daddy?"

Idgie cleared her throat, reached in her shirt pocket, and pulled out a Lucky Strike cigarette. "Oh . . . I may have run into him a couple of times, why?"

Then he asked the very question she had been hoping to avoid. "I wonder why he never comes to see me."

"Reach over and hand me a match, will ya? Gosh, I don't know, honey. Did you ever ask your momma about it?"

"No ma'am. She doesn't like to talk about him. I don't think she likes him very much."

Idgie hoped he would drop the subject, but he didn't.

"Do you think he might come to see me sometime?"

Idgie looked over at him. "Would you like that?"

Buddy said. "I think I would . . . but I don't know . . . maybe. It's my birthday next week. Do you think he might call me, or maybe send me a present?"

"I don't know, honey."

After a little while, they were driving over the downtown viaduct when he asked another question.

"I wonder where he is right now, Aunt Idgie."

"Who?"

"My dad."

"Oh . . . I really don't know." Then, quickly changing the subject, Idgie said, "Hey, Buddy, I've got a great idea. You're getting old enough now. You need to learn to shoot. Me and Cleo and a few of the boys are going on a hunting trip next weekend. How 'bout you come with us?"

Buddy's eyes lit up. "Can I? Will Momma let me?"

"Sure. Leave it to me, I'll fix it with her. What d'you say? Will you come?"

"You bet."

IDGIE HATED LIKE hell to lie to Buddy, but she didn't have the heart to tell him the truth about his father. Frank Bennett was a mean drunk and a wife beater. When he and Ruth were married, he had beaten poor Ruth so many times that finally Momma and Poppa Threadgoode had sent Idgie with Big George and Julian over to Georgia to get Ruth out of there before he wound up killing her in one of his drunken rages. But Buddy didn't need to know about all that. The less he knew about him, the better.

MUCH TO IDGIE'S relief, even after his mother died, he never asked about his father again. And as the years went by with no word from him, Buddy just considered himself a member of the Threadgoode family, and that was that.

A New Friend

THE NEXT DAY, while Ruthie was having a facial, Evelyn was over at the hospital visiting with Bud and talking to him about Ninny. She said, "You know, Bud . . . may I call you Bud?"

"I'd be hurt if you didn't."

"Anyhow, Bud, it's funny how just one person can change your entire life. When I first met Ninny, I was going through just a terrible time. I was depressed, having crazy thoughts. And I hate to say it, but I'd even thought about killing myself. It scares me to think about all I would have missed if I had."

"Yeah. Meeting me for one."

Evelyn smiled. "That's right. Of course, looking back now, I could have been going through some kind of a nervous breakdown. Now, I'm not a religious person, but sometimes, Bud, I believe Ninny must have been some sort of an angel sent to me, to help me get through that time and come out the other side. And don't think I'm crazy, but I wouldn't be surprised if she had something to do with my meeting you and Ruthie."

"No, I don't think you're crazy at all. I believe it. I think people, even though they have gone on, still look out for us when we need it."

"You do?"

"Yes, I do. Something happened to me once. I never told anybody before, but I'll tell you. Shut the door first. I don't want Terry to hear us. She might have us both committed to the psych ward."

Evelyn closed the door, and sat back down.

"Well, in 1989, when Aunt Idgie died, it really hit me hard. I took her back home to Alabama to bury her in the family plot like she wanted, but the next day, before I left, I went back to the cemetery to say goodbye one more time. I was standing at her gravestone, crying and carrying on, and feeling oh-so-sorry for myself. My mother was gone. Aunt Idgie was gone. I was now a sixty-year-old orphan. Oh, woe is me. And right at that very moment, I'll be darned if a damn bee didn't fly right up my pant leg and sting me in the behind."

"No."

"Yes ma'am, he did, and he stung the hell out of me, too. So after I got over the shock of it, it suddenly dawned on me. It had been Aunt Idgie who sent that bee up my pants. She wanted to let me know that she was just fine, and to quit carrying on and feeling so sorry for myself. So, I sat right down on her grave and started laughing so hard that I fell over in the grass. And I couldn't stop. I just lay there in the cemetery for a good half hour, rolling around in the grass, all by myself, laughing my head off. If anybody had seen me that day they really would have thought I was crazy. I tell you, Aunt Idgie was just a devil, doing that to me. But you know, Evelyn, the funny thing is, after that day I never had that painful grieving anymore. I missed her, of course, but I knew she was all right.

"So my point is, Aunt Ninny may very well have had a hand in your meeting the two of us. And just between us, my Ruthie needs a friend right now. She hasn't had an easy time lately, losing her husband, and now me causing her all this trouble. I hope you two will stay in touch. After we leave, I sure hope that maybe you'll give her a call once in a while."

The Weems Weekly

(WHISTLE STOP, ALABAMA'S WEEKLY BULLETIN)

1947

LOCAL FOOTBALL STAR!

WE HAVE SOME happy news this week. We are so proud of home-town boy Buddy Threadgoode leading our football team to state victory. Just heard he was named Alabama high school quarter-back of the year. He credits his Aunt Idgie for teaching him how to throw a football when he was only seven. We hear our boy may be on his way to Georgia Tech next year.

On a sadder note: Even though it has been only a few months, all of us in Whistle Stop continue to be heartbroken over losing our dear Ruth Jamison. It's still so hard to walk in the cafe and not see her greeting us, as she always did, with her beautiful welcom-ing smile. Idgie and Buddy send thanks to all of you for your gen-erous donations. Grace over at the humane society says that so many donations were made in Ruth's name that they have built a new room in the back for the cats and raccoons. The old one was just too small. Knowing Ruth, I am sure she would have loved that.

. . . Dot Weems . . .

Whistle Stop, Alabama

1955

WHEN RUTH DIED, Idgie'd had to hold herself together for Buddy's sake. He needed her to be strong. She had wanted to close the cafe then, but she couldn't. She needed the money. She had made a solemn promise to Ruth that no matter what, she would make sure that Buddy finished college.

Buddy had taken his mother's death pretty hard. It had happened in his senior year of high school. However, the next fall, after he left Whistle Stop for college and got busy making new friends, things changed for the better. But not for Idgie.

Every evening after the cafe closed, Idgie would grab a bottle of whiskey from under the counter, get in her car, and drive all night long. She would speed seventy or eighty miles an hour, flying up and down dark country roads, her radio blaring, drunk as a loon, singing at the top of her lungs.

It was as if the speed, the noise, and the booze could somehow help numb the pain. And it did for a few hours, but then every dawn, when she got back home, she still had to face another day without Ruth. Another day of hating God for taking her away.

But later, after Buddy graduated from college and was on his way to a great life, Idgie felt she had kept her promise to Ruth. And now what? The town was falling apart, all her railroad pals had left, everyone else was leaving or getting ready to. Her older sister Leona had just written to her wondering whether they should sell the old two-story Threadgoode family house, since nobody was living there anymore. Idgie really didn't have a reason to stay, and every reason to take off. The cafe held too many memories. Besides, she had just spent a rough night in jail over in Gate City, for speeding and drunk driving. She had to get out of town before one of these nights she killed herself, or even worse, someone else. Her friend Sheriff Grady had made a call to her brother Julian in Florida, and told him that everybody was worried about Idgie. She was just not herself anymore. He told Julian, "You better do something soon, 'cause I don't know if I can get her outta jail the next time. Especially if she takes another swing at some cop that's tryin' to arrest her." Julian immediately called Idgie and told her to get herself down to Florida now, or if not he would come up and get her.

A week later, when Idgie pulled up to his house and got out, Julian was shocked at her appearance. She was bone thin, looked terrible, and reeked of whiskey and cigarettes. She fell down twice before he could even get her into the house. The next morning, after she'd had a few cups of coffee, Idgie's hands were shaking and she was sweating and pale as a ghost, but she was at least halfway sober. So Julian started in on her. "Grady called and told me a friend of his over in Gate City had clocked you doing ninety-five miles an hour at four o'clock in the morning. Do you realize you could have killed yourself drinking and driving like some kind of maniac?"

"I don't care . . . wish I had."

"My God, Idgie. I know you lost your best friend, but you're actin' like a damn fool, getting yourself thrown in jail like that. What in hell are you thinking?"

She looked at him, for a long time. Then she said, "Ruth was more than a best friend, Julian."

Julian was a little surprised to hear her say so, but he just nodded. "I know that, Idgie. I just don't see how killing yourself over it is going to help matters. We all lose people, Idgie. That's life. I love you, but you aren't special. You're just another human being who lost somebody they loved. I'm your brother, don't you care about me? I don't want to lose my little sister. And I'll tell you another thing. Ruth would be ashamed of the way you're acting. Sure, you miss her. We all do, but is this any way to honor her memory? And if you don't care about yourself or me, at least think about Buddy. You're the only parent he has left. Do you think he wants some drunk old woman showing up at his wedding? You need to stop this nonsense now. Do you hear me?"

Idgie had heard what he said. And he'd made a point. Ruth had been a lady, and she would have been ashamed of her.

THAT NIGHT SHE found herself sitting next to Julian in an AA meeting. After Idgie joined Alcoholics Anonymous, her life began to change. She found a female sponsor to help her with the Twelve Steps, and Idgie actually did what the woman said to do. Her sponsor was a tough old Florida gal who didn't let her get away with a thing, and, being so stubborn, Idgie needed that. In the following weeks, she met an awful lot of nice people that were just like her. People who had been through hell and back, trying to move forward to a better future.

Idgie found that she actually loved going to the meetings and getting to know everybody. It was almost like living in a small community again. She still missed Whistle Stop, but she knew there was nothing there for her anymore.

It took a while, but eventually Idgie even started to believe in something again. It wasn't the same exact faith she'd had as a child, but it seemed to work.

After a few years of being sober, Idgie started sponsoring new-comers herself, and some old-timers as well. You couldn't drive by the fruit stand without seeing someone sitting outside with her, talking to her. Of course, she still missed Ruth as much as ever, but at least she was not killing herself or anybody else over it any-more. She didn't have time. She was kept pretty busy these days at the fruit stand and tending to her beehives and, as she put it, "Just doing my little bit for mankind."

Surprise Visitors

JUST AFTER RUTHIE and Evelyn left the hospital that afternoon, Nurse Terry knocked on Bud's door and walked in.

"Hey, Mr. Popular. You have a couple more visitors."

Bud looked up and was surprised to see Billy Hornbeck, his friend from the train, walk in with a young lady.

"Billy, my boy! Hey, what a nice surprise. How are you?"

"Just fine, sir. How are you?"

"Fit as a fiddle. How did you know I was here?"

"It was in the papers. I hope you don't mind my coming. I just wanted to check up on you. You should have told me you wanted to go to Whistle Stop. I would have been happy to take you."

Bud laughed. "Well, Billy, I didn't know I wanted to go myself, until I got to Birmingham. But I never did find it, and not only that, I lost my arm out in the woods."

"Yes sir, I noticed it was missing. But at least you're okay."

"I am, and it's really sweet of you to come and check up on me."

"No problem. But the other reason I came is that I wanted you to meet Geena."

The young woman standing with Billy stepped up and said, "How do you do, sir," while shaking his hand firmly. "Pleased to meet you."

"Same here, Geena." Bud looked at Billy. "Is this the fireperson you told me about?"

"Yes sir," he said, beaming at her.

"So, Geena. I know you are not supposed to tell a fire-person they are pretty, but you sure are."

"Thank you, sir."

After they had visited a while, Terry came back in and said, "Sorry, folks, but we have to get this guy up to physical therapy."

"Oh, that's all right," Billy said. "We were just leaving."

"Well, I guess I'll have to do what she says. She beats me up if I don't. But thanks so much for coming, you two. Great to meet you, Geena."

"Same here, Mr. Threadgoode. Sorry you lost your arm."

As they went out the door, Billy stuck his head back in for a second and said, "The wedding's back on."

Bud gave him the victory sign. "Good for you, boy."

Bud then turned to Terry and said, "Ain't love grand?"

"I wouldn't know. . . . I'm married."

Going Back to Briarwood

THE NEXT MORNING, Ruthie and Evelyn came to the hospital at around eight to pick Bud up.

When Ruthie opened the closet to help him get dressed for the trip home, she was appalled.

"Oh, Daddy. Don't tell me you wore this old worn-out jacket in public. You told me you got rid of it."

"I did? I don't remember."

"And look at your good pants. They have grass stains all over them. Oh well, there's nothing to be done now."

After Bud was checked out of the hospital, Terry wheeled him downstairs and waited while Evelyn brought the car around to the front door. When she pulled up, Terry helped get Bud get into the car and said, "You take care of yourself, or I'll have to come over to Atlanta and give you what-for, you hear?"

"Okay, I'll try," said Bud. "And you tell that husband of yours to watch out, or I might come over here and steal you."

After Bud was in the car and the door was shut, Ruthie said, "Terry, thanks so much for taking such good care of him. You've just been an angel."

"Well . . . he's easy to take care of. He's a real sweetheart."

LATER, AS EVELYN stood in the airport watching Ruthie and Bud's plane take off, she realized she was going to miss them. She had known them for only a few days, but it had been so nice to finally meet someone who had also known Ninny.

WHEN RUTHIE AND Bud landed back in Atlanta and were waiting for her car at the parking lot, Ruthie turned to Bud. "Daddy, are you sure you won't come home with me? You know you don't have to go back to Briarwood if you don't want to."

Bud shook his head "No, no, honey. Your mother-in-law would be upset if I left. And besides, I'm used to the place now. I'll just go back and take my medicine. I guess I will have to apologize to Merris, though."

"If you're planning to stay, it might be a good idea."

When they drove up to Briarwood Manor, Mr. Merris was waiting in the front entrance with a flower in his lapel and a pained smile plastered on his face.

"Well, here is our wandering boy. Welcome back, Mr. Threadgoode."

"Thank you. Yes . . . listen, I'm sorry about the little mishap. I sort of—"

Thankfully at that moment, Bud's friend Hattie came down the hall toward them and called out, "Hey, Mr. Threadgoode, I hear you took a trip on a train, and I want to hear all about it. Come on with me, your room is all ready for you."

Ruthie waited outside in the car until she knew everything was all right. It must have been, because Bud turned around and gave her a little wave, and he was smiling.

After she had dropped her father off, Ruthie drove across town to her house. When she arrived at the big iron gate, she punched in the code and drove into the Circle. She had left home with only a purse, but had returned with a suitcase that Evelyn Couch had lent her, filled with Mary Kay products and some new clothes she'd bought in Birmingham.

She was headed into her house when, across the way, Martha Lee opened her front door, looked at her, then went back in and shut the door.

As soon as Ruthie walked inside, her phone was ringing.

"I see you are finally home," said Martha Lee.

"Yes, I am. I stayed a little longer than I'd planned."

"And your father? Is he back as well?"

"Yes, I just dropped him off."

"I hope you are aware that his behavior was quite an embarrassment, not only to me, but to the Manor."

Ruthie closed her eyes and silently sighed. "Yes. I'm sure it must have been. Daddy said to apologize to you, and tell you that it won't happen again."

"I hope not. Also, were you aware that when you ran out like that, without a word to me or the staff, that you left your stove on? If Ramón had not gone in to check on things, you could have burned down the entire Circle."

"No, I wasn't aware. I'm sorry."

After Ruthie hung up, she said to herself, "Welcome home, Ruthie." Before she could get upstairs, the phone rang again.

"Listen, you'd better call Carolyn right away and tell her you're home. She's been extremely upset over her grandfather's behavior."

"Yes, I will do that, thank you."

Ruthie would call, but not right away. She knew she would get another lecture. Carolyn and Martha Lee were always on the same page.

Jessie Ray Scroggins

1978

JESSIE RAY SCROGGINS was one of the many kids in Whistle Stop that Idgie would pile into a car and take to the picture show every Saturday. He was a handful, always getting into trouble, fighting in the back seat, throwing popcorn at people in the theater, but Idgie liked him.

Being a preacher's son was never easy, particularly in a small town. And doubly hard, if you were a son of Reverend Robert A. Scroggins, minister at the Whistle Stop Baptist Church, where a sign on the young adults Bible study blackboard read: WE DON'T DRINK, SMOKE, OR DANCE, OR DATE THOSE WHO DO.

JESSIE RAY HAD come out of the womb wriggling like a worm, and he never stopped wriggling. He seemed to have been given a double dose of energy. The minute he could stand up, he didn't walk, he ran. From the time he was five, the first thing his poor mother had to do every morning was open the door and let him run out in the yard, or else he would have broken everything she had. His older brother, Bobby Scroggins, had gotten into trouble a few times for drinking too much, but Bobby had gone on to become a successful lawyer. Jessie Ray was a different story.

Jessie Ray had been given his first drink when he was ten by a friend of Idgie's named Smokey Lonesome who used to hang out at the cafe. And he'd liked it right away. Not the taste, but the way it had made him feel. And the more he drank the better he felt. By the time he was eighteen, he had wrecked three cars and been in jail in Birmingham five times.

Each time, he had called Idgie and she'd driven over and bailed him out. She was the only person in Whistle Stop he could call who wouldn't tell his daddy.

Jessie Ray had gone into the army, and his daddy had hoped it would make a man out of him. However, when he came home from Korea, after having seen so many of his army buddies get killed, he seemed to be worse. As hard as he tried, he could not stop drinking. He knew he was letting his parents, his wife, his friends, and everybody else down, but there was a part of him that didn't want to live.

He had given up on himself as a hopeless case, and then one night in a drunken stupor he called Idgie down in Florida and talked to her for almost two hours, telling her how he was going to kill himself. All he remembered of the conversation was the last thing she'd said: "Jessie Ray, you get your sorry-ass self down here right now!"

His father had tried everything. Maybe, just maybe, Idgie could do something with him. Nobody else could. The following day, his daddy drove Jessie down to Florida, let him out of the car, and drove off. The next thing Jessie knew he was sitting in an AA meeting, with Idgie on one side of him and her brother Julian on the other.

It took a while. He had a few setbacks. But slowly he began to understand himself a little better. For as long as he could remember, he had always felt uncomfortable in his own skin. The only relief he could find was in the bottle. He figured out later that this must be why they called it "spirits." After about six months, when he was sober, healthy, and tan from picking oranges, Idgie sent him back home to his wife and kids, pretty much a changed man.

Jessie found out that being sober was wonderful, but it could also be painful at times, especially when he had to have the big LIFE SUCKS tattoo removed from his chest. It had hurt like hell, but nothing like having to face the fact that his daddy had died before he'd gotten a chance to tell him how sorry he was for all the hurt he'd caused. A few years later, hoping to do some good in what life he had left, he became a minister and took over his father's church in Birmingham. Although his daddy had been hardshell Baptist, Jessie leaned more toward a nondenominational point of view.

At first, he faced some resistance from the older Bible-based members. Some people remembered Jessie's bad behavior, and there were complaints that he was a little too loosey-goosey with his preaching. But with a little effort, he soon found plenty of appropriate Bible verses that filled the bill and everyone came back into the fold.

Word spread about what good, positive sermons he was giving and soon there were not enough seats in the small church. He was having to do an eight, nine, and eleven o'clock service to get all the people in.

When the big Piggly Wiggly supermarket at the old Eastwood Mall closed, Jessie saw his chance and quickly rented out the space. Within three years he had created a megachurch that seated over five thousand. His Sunday service had become so popular that soon it was broadcast live over WBRC-TV, right after the *Country Boy Eddie* show.

Safe at the Plate

BIRMINGHAM, ALABAMA
1982

OPAL BUTTS HAD called her old friend Gladys Kilgore in Tennessee, and they were catching up on the latest news about the old Whistle Stop gang. Gladys was astonished at what she heard.

"Jessie Ray Scroggins is now a preacher? Why, Grady must have arrested that boy over twenty times. You have got to be fooling me."

"No, I'm not. After Reverend Scroggins died, Jessie Ray got himself some kind of minister's license and took over his daddy's congregation. And at first people were a little leery about going, given his criminal record and all, so he started out real slow, but over time he's built himself quite a following. So many people were coming that there weren't enough seats to fit everybody. Now he's preaching over at the old Piggly Wiggly supermarket building, right up the street from me."

"You're kiddin' me."

"No. I go every Sunday. It still feels a little weird to be worshipping in the same place where I used to buy my produce, but he's an awful good preacher, Gladys. He puts out a good, positive, things-to-live-by message, and you always feel good when you leave."

After she hung up, Gladys was still in a state of shock. "Jessie

Ray Scroggins? A preacher at the Piggly Wiggly supermarket?" But she guessed it must be true. You couldn't make that up if you tried.

JESSIE RAY HAD been clean and sober ever since he came back from Florida, and had completely turned his life around. He had his church, his wife and children back, and was doing great. But they say that no matter how long you are sober, you can still have a slip.

One night, Jessie Ray found himself sitting in a neighborhood bar. He suddenly realized he was drunk. And he knew he had to get home right away. He somehow found his car keys and stumbled to his car. He was almost home, only a few blocks away, but as drunk as he was, he still felt a slight thump as he drove over it. He must have hit a speed bump.

The next morning the police were at his door, and he was being arrested for a hit-and-run felony. That slight bump had been the body of a ten-year-old boy he'd run over and killed. As the police were handcuffing him and dragging him to the squad car, he started screaming at the top of his lungs for his wife. "Help! Help!"

Then Jessie suddenly woke up, bathed from head to toe in a cold sweat with his heart pounding. He sat up in bed, gasping for air, and realized it had been a dream. He kept repeating, "It was just a dream. It was just a dream. I'm still sober! Thank you, God. Thank you, Idgie." He quickly threw back his covers and jumped out of bed, and ran into the kitchen to give his wife a great big hug. He hadn't gotten drunk. He hadn't run over a little boy after all. He was not going to jail today.

Evelyn and Ruthie

OFTEN PEOPLE SAY "Let's keep in touch," and then don't. This was not the case with Evelyn and Ruthie. After their short time together when Bud was in the hospital, they called and chatted with each other almost every day. A few times Ruthie even went over and spent the weekend with Evelyn in Birmingham, and Evelyn would sometimes drive over to Pine Mountain, Georgia, not far from Atlanta, and meet Ruthie for lunch. And as friends get closer, they start to tell each other everything.

Today Ruthie was telling Evelyn about her daughter, Carolyn Lee. "Now, I love her, but we have never been very close. Certainly not as close as I would like. Carolyn can be . . . well . . . a little shallow. But I blame that on Martha Lee and her influence on Carolyn. Anyhow, it's a disappointment. I've tried. But when we do get together, all she really wants to talk about is what outfit she is going to wear to the next party, or the important people she has met.

"Her husband, Brian, is a nice boy, but they're both caught up in the Washington social life, always going from one party to the next. I just hope that the marriage holds up, because if Carolyn was ever thrown into the real world . . . I worry. Now, my son, Richard, is, well, he's cut from a different cloth than Carolyn. He's his own person, and he was always pretty much that way. When he was younger, I asked him what he wanted to be when he grew up, and he said, "I'm not sure yet, Mother, but I do know I don't want to be unhappy."

Evelyn said, "Wow, I wish I'd been that smart. When I was young, I always knew what everybody else wanted me to be, I was clear on that. And both of my children seemed to always know what they wanted to be, and they went out and did it. But I never knew what I wanted until I met Ninny and started working at age forty-eight. But what about you, Ruthie? What did you want to be?"

"Oh, gosh, Evelyn, you're going to laugh if I tell you. It's so lame."

"No, I won't."

"Well, when I was younger, I was always kinda shy. But there was this restaurant in Baltimore where we used to go for special occasions, and when you walked in, this beautiful lady would greet you at the door and make you feel so welcome, and escort you to your table."

"Like a hostess?"

"Yes, I guess that's what you would call it, a hostess. Anyhow, at the time I thought she must have the most glamorous job in the world, looking pretty, greeting people, making them feel special. Isn't that the dumbest thing you ever heard?"

Evelyn shook her head. "No, not at all. Hey, when I was sixteen I wanted to be a nun, and I'm not even Catholic."

"Oh, for heaven's sake," said Ruthie. "Just think, I could be here talking to Sister Evelyn, or, knowing you, Pope Evelyn the First."

Fairhope, Alabama

CHRISTMAS 1997

From: DotWeems@hotmail.com

Hey gang,

I hope you got my last one. I am still not sure how well this email thing works. I keep pushing the wrong button. Hard to teach an old dog new tricks, I guess.

So, another year and we are still alive and kicking. The highlight of our year was that our old friend Opal Butts, who was on her way to Florida, stopped by here to say hello. She is still as pretty as ever! Remember in 1927 when Opal was crowned Miss Whistle Stop and represented us in the Miss Alabama contest and we all went to cheer her on?

We still think she was robbed. How many girls do you know who can tap-dance and play the spoons at the same time? No matter who won, Opal will always be our Miss Alabama.

By the way, don't you miss all the good old movie stars? I do. We saw *Pillow Talk* on the classic movie channel last night. What a hoot. And they just don't make movie stars like Fred and Ginger anymore. Try as I may, I can't seem to get excited about the new ones. I don't even know their names and couldn't tell you one from another. I guess it happens to us all. My mother had been wild-eyed about a heartthrob named Rudolph Valentino. "Who's he?" I remember asking. See what I mean?

Had to take Wilbur to the emergency room in May. The crazy fool was out on the pier feeding the seagulls by hand, and one of them missed the oyster cracker he was holding up and nicked his nose instead. Needless to say, he was not a pretty sight with the big bandage on his nose, but it's all healed up now.

By the way, speaking of unexpected things, I had a rude awakening at the doctor's this year. The gal taking my weight and height told me that I was five foot three and I said, "No, that's not right. I'm five feet four and a half, and I've always been five feet four and a half." I made her measure again, and sure enough she was right. Gang, I have shrunk! No wonder my pants are too long. It's me! I'm too short.

But on a happier note: Did you know that once you pass seventy-five and you are still alive, it means you have a better than average chance on making it past ninety? So let's keep on going! The way they are curing all these diseases and replacing body parts left and right, who knows, we could live forever. My question is, would you want to? Write and tell me what you think.

Well, signing off for another year. They tell us it's not PC to say Merry Christmas anymore, but Merry Christmas anyway, everybody!

Your faithful scribe,

Dot

Opal Butts

OPAL BUTTS HAD three sisters, Ruby, Pearl, and the baby, Garnet. It was clear her mother had been hung up on jewelry. And Opal had been hung up on fixing hair since she was eighteen. After she married Julian Threadgoode, she started a small beauty shop in their kitchen. It might have been one of the reasons for their divorce. Every time he came home, there were at least three women in the kitchen and two more in the living room, chatting away, waiting to get their hair fixed. All weekend, there were women in and out of the house at all hours, and it had driven Julian crazy. Finally, he gave Opal an ultimatum and she chose the beauty business. After he moved down to Florida, she opened up her own beauty shop two doors down from the cafe and was very successful.

But in 1954, Opal had to close her beauty shop in Whistle Stop, and wound up moving to Birmingham and working for a beauty shop in a downtown hotel. It was so different. At her own shop she had known all of her customers, but now the customers were mostly walk-ins. And almost nobody wanted a permanent wave anymore.

But Opal's main preoccupation now was heading up her condo association, and the job was turning out to be extremely stressful.

So stressful, she had just ordered a T-shirt that read KILL ME IF I EVER VOLUNTEER AGAIN. The main problem was that her neighborhood was in flux. As the older residents left, young singles were moving in, and the atmosphere was changing. And oh, how the singles loved to party. Now that it was summer, every weekend at the pool, someone was having a cookout and playing loud music, and who did everyone call to complain? Opal was so tired of having to get up out of bed, go out, and ask them to turn down the music and keep their voices down. They were usually pretty good about it, but within an hour, it was just as loud. Sometimes she had to call the police to get them to be quiet.

Noise was one thing. She understood they were just trying to have a good time, but these kids had all kinds of people showing up at their parties. People they didn't know. A lot of the older residents were worried that some of these strangers might come back and rob them. It was a valid fear. There had been a lot of holdups and carjackings going on lately.

One night just last week she had stayed late at work. A group of girls, in town for a bachelorette party, came into the salon pretty drunk and wanted her to dye their hair pink to match their dresses for the wedding, and they didn't leave the shop until after ten that night.

She had closed up the shop and was walking to her car when she noticed a scruffy-looking man in a long coat who seemed to be following her. She looked around the parking lot, and most of the cars were gone. When she realized she was alone, she began to walk a little faster, and so did he. She was now convinced this guy was up to no good. Oh Lord, he was probably going to rob her and steal her car or worse. She didn't know, all she knew was she had to think fast.

As she got a little closer to her car, she slowly reached inside her beauty supply bag, pulled out a curling iron, then quickly turned and pointed it at him. And in the deepest and loudest voice she could manage, she growled, "You come one step closer, sucker, and I'll blow your head off."

It must have scared him, because he backed off and went the other way. As she stood there and watched him leave she felt just like John Wayne, and, boy, did that feel good. That bastard wasn't going to get her tip money, not tonight. Not as hard as she'd worked.

The Birthday Wish

IT WAS HER father's eighty-fifth birthday, and Ruthie had invited Evelyn to come over to Atlanta and have dinner with them as a little surprise for him. Evelyn was delighted. She really liked Bud, and enjoyed talking about the old days in Whistle Stop. It was almost like being with Ninny again.

THAT AFTERNOON, RUTHIE picked Evelyn up at the airport, and as they were turning in to Caldwell Circle, Ruthie said, "Evelyn, look over at the big house. Do you see a face in the window yet?"

Evelyn looked. "No, not yet."

"Well, keep looking." And as they got out of the car, a curtain was suddenly pulled aside in one of the upstairs windows, and a face peered out. Ruthie said, "There she is, right on schedule." Ruthie faked a quick little smile and waved at her, and the face quickly disappeared behind the curtain.

"Who was that?"

"My mother-in-law."

Evelyn said, "Oh dear, I knew she lived close by, but not that close. She really is right on top of you, isn't she?"

"Oh yes, and in more ways than one." As they entered the

house, Ruthie stopped in the entrance hall and said, "Hold on a minute, Evelyn," then walked over to the house phone and waited. Five seconds later, it rang. Ruthie rolled her eyes and answered.

"Hello, Martha."

"I see we have a visitor."

"Yes, we do."

Ruthie counted to five on her fingers, and waited.

"Do I know her?"

"No, I don't think so, Martha," she said, looking at Evelyn. "She's an old friend of mine from Alabama."

"Oh, I see. Well, have a nice day," she said and hung up. Ruthie shook her head. "Sorry. Anyhow, come on in; this is home, such as it is."

Evelyn put her bag down, walked around the living room, and peeked into the dining room. "Oh, Ruthie, this place is just beautiful. And these colors. I just love this shade of yellow on the walls, and all these gorgeous slipcovers, and your rugs. Who was your decorator?"

Ruthie shrugged. "Just me."

"You did all of this by yourself?"

"Yes, it was a hard-fought battle getting rid of all the big, dark antique furniture Martha Lee had in here, but it was one battle I won, thank heavens."

"I should say so. I had to hire an army of people to do my house."

"Of course, it took a while. I had to replace the wallpaper and put in all new light fixtures."

"Well, you did a great job. You have a real talent, Ruthie."

"Why, thank you, Evelyn."

"You must entertain a lot."

"No, not really. We used to, but when Brooks died, most of our friends were married couples, and when you're suddenly a single woman, your life changes. But I do miss the fun we all used to have."

That night, Ruthie dropped Evelyn off at the restaurant and then picked up her father at Briarwood Manor. Bud had assumed it would just be the two of them, but when he walked in and saw Evelyn sitting at the table, his eyes lit up. "Well, look who's here. It's my friend Evelyn. What a great surprise!"

They had a festive evening talking about the old days, and Bud said, "Hey, Evelyn, did Ninny ever tell you about the time Aunt Idgie shot that guy who was trying to kill her cat?"

"No."

"Or the times when she and my mother threw all the government food off the train to the poor sharecroppers?"

"Yes, she did tell me that. But tell me again."

Ruthie sat back and listened as Bud told a story she'd heard at least a hundred times, but she was just so happy to see him having such a good time.

Later, as they were taking him back to Briarwood, Bud said, "Thanks for spending my birthday with us, Evelyn. Let's do it again next year!"

Evelyn said, "You bet, Bud. I've already got it down on my calendar."

Bud got out of the car and walked up to the front door, then turned around and waved goodbye. As she waved back, Ruthie said, "Oh, Evelyn, sometimes he just breaks my heart. I know he's lonesome. But he's so brave, never complains, always tries to be cheerful. But I think that's the reason he tried to find Whistle Stop again. He really misses home."

"I'm sure he does. I see how he lights up when we talk about it."

"Oh yes, and the sad part is, his home's not even there anymore, and there's not a thing I can do about it."

"It is sad. But, Ruthie, don't forget, he has you. And as he says, you really are the best daughter in the world. That cake you ordered for him tonight was just beautiful."

Ruthie smiled. "It was, wasn't it? But have you ever seen so many candles on one cake in your life? I thought the poor waiter would never get them all lit."

"It was a lot of candles," said Evelyn. "But God bless him, he blew them out. Every last one of them. I wonder what he wished for?"

Ruthie shook her head. "I don't know, Evelyn. Another year maybe?"

"Well, whatever it was, I hope he gets it."

BUD HAD MADE a birthday wish that night, but it hadn't been for him. It had been for Ruthie. He wished that she would find something or someone to make her happy again.

Dot Weems

FAIRHOPE, ALABAMA

January 1988

I am sure that by now you have all heard about Big George's passing. His daughter, Alberta, who is now a chef in Birmingham, called us with the sad news. He will be missed. Nobody could barbecue like Big George. Alberta said he was still cooking right up to the end.

On a happier note, Wilbur and I spent our New Year's Eve over at the Elks Club, and I won twenty-five dollars in the fill-your-card bingo game. That was a very nice way to start off the new year. I am also happy to report that Wilbur survived his second childhood moment. This is the story of why I have twenty more gray hairs today.

The kids that live next door to us got a huge trampoline for Christmas and have it sitting out in their yard. And lo and behold the next morning while I was washing my breakfast dishes, I happened to look out the window just in time to see my crazy husband bouncing up and down at least six feet in the air! I tell you, it liked to have scared me to death. Needless to say I dropped everything and ran out and made him come down off that thing. Men! No matter how old they are, they never grow up, do they? The old fool could have broken every bone in his body. He said he had a lot of fun bouncing on that thing, but it was no fun for me. I could have been a widow today if I hadn't stopped him. Honestly, folks, I just never know what he will do next. Oh well, can't live with him, can't live without him. I guess I'll just live with him and hope he doesn't give me a heart attack next time. And so, until next time, don't take any foolish chances, because life is too short as it is. Just remember, no matter what time it is, it's always later than you think.

Your faithful scribe,
Dot

The Proposal

ON RUTHIE'S NEXT trip over to Birmingham, she and Evelyn went to the same restaurant where they had gone the first night they'd met, over a year before. After they ordered, Evelyn asked Ruthie how her dad was doing.

"Oh, the same, I guess. But he always asks about you. He's so glad we are friends."

"Me, too." Suddenly Evelyn thought of something and called the waiter over. "Bring us a nice big bottle of champagne, will you?"

Ruthie said, "Champagne? Are we celebrating something?"

"You never know. We might be."

When the waiter brought the champagne and began pouring it, Evelyn said, "Ruthie I have a proposal for you."

"What?"

"You know that I was an only child."

"You told me. So was I."

"But for as long as I can remember, I always wished I had a sister."

"So did I."

"So . . . Ruthie Threadgoode, will you be my little sister? The one I never had?"

Tears suddenly welled up in Ruthie's eyes.

"Yes, of course I will, and will you, Evelyn Couch, be my big sister?"

"I will."

Evelyn picked up her glass and said, "Let's make a toast. To my new little sister, Ruthie."

Ruthie picked up hers and said, "To Evelyn, the best big sister I could ever have."

The idea of getting a sister so late in life touched them so much they both starting crying. Then, embarrassed to be crying, they began laughing and crying at the same time.

Their waiter saw the tears and came over to the table, concerned that something was wrong, and said, "Pardon me, but are you ladies all right?"

Evelyn looked up and said, "Oh yes, we are just fine," but as she was busy reassuring him nothing was wrong, she knocked over her glass and spilled what was left of her champagne in her lap. Then Evelyn and Ruthie both burst out laughing so loud that people all over the restaurant started staring at them.

Evelyn looked around and said, "Uh-oh. We'd better behave ourselves or they're going to throw us out of here on our ear."

Ruthie quickly put on a serious face and said, "Okay, Sis." And then after a few seconds they both burst out laughing again.

The waiter, now back in the kitchen, looking out of the small round window into the dining room, said to the chef, "Oh, man, Mrs. Couch is sure tying one on tonight."

The chef said, "Good. The drunker they are, the bigger the tip."

The chef was right. That hundred-dollar bill Evelyn left was much appreciated.

A Close Call

IT WAS THAT time of the year again when Reverend Scroggins would take all of his church workers over to Columbus, Georgia, to the big summer Baptist Bible camp for the entire weekend. Ruth had gone with the others to help serve food, and she'd taken Buddy with her. While they were away, Idgie decided to get Big George to bring the boat down to the river so they could go fishing for catfish. Ruth didn't care much for catfish, but Idgie and Big George did.

Early the next morning, after they got the boat into the water, they headed out with their fishing tackle, a shotgun, and two bacon sandwiches apiece that Sipsey had made.

An hour later, Big George was slowly rowing the boat close to the bank of the river, hoping to catch another one of the big mud cats that liked to feed there. They already had six big ones in the bucket.

As they passed under the limb of a large tree, they suddenly heard a loud thump and felt a slight jolt. Something heavy had fallen off of the tree and into the boat. Idgie hadn't seen what it was, but Big George had. In a very calm and low voice he said, "Miss Idgie, don't move. Don't you move a muscle," as he slowly reached for the shotgun. Idgie looked down in time to see a huge water moccasin at her feet with its mouth wide open, getting ready to strike.

That very second, Big George pulled the trigger and blasted a large black hole in the bottom of the boat, taking the shattered hull and what was left of the snake down with it. As the boat began to sink, they both had to swim over to the bank and pull themselves out of the river.

Big George had destroyed the boat, but he had also saved her life. A bite from a cottonmouth was deadly poisonous and probably would have killed her faster than he could have gotten her to a hospital.

They were both sopping wet as they walked back to the car and Idgie said, "I didn't like that old boat much anyway, did you?"

Big George laughed. "That's good, because it's on the bottom of the river now. Along with all them fish we caught, too."

"Yeah, that's right. But I'm just glad you're a good shot. Anyone else might have shot my foot off."

"I tried not to."

"Whew . . . He was a big ole boy, wasn't he?"

"That he was. Five to six pounds I'd reckon."

MOST PEOPLE WOULD have panicked at the sight of a big snake like that so close to them, but, thankfully, Big George wasn't afraid of snakes. Working outside in the backwoods, he had handled a lot of snakes in his day.

But then, Big George was kind of fearless when he had to be. He'd once jumped into a hog pen and saved a three-year-old child who had fallen in. And as everybody knew, hogs will attack and eat anything, and Big George still had the scars on his arms to prove it.

After they'd dried off with some old rags, Big George left in his truck to go back home, and Idgie got back into her car to follow him. But before she did she pulled out the bottle of whiskey she kept hidden under the seat and took a few swigs. Coming that close to being bitten by that snake today had really shaken her up. As she sat there, she started thinking about how unpredictable life is. One moment you're alive, and the next one you could be dead.

She took another swig. Idgie had promised Ruth on the Bible that she would never go back down to the River Club. But, on the other hand, Ruth wouldn't be back from Bible camp until tomorrow. And Idgie sure didn't feel like going home right now. It was just up the road a bit. Maybe she would stop by for just one drink. What could one little drink hurt?

THE RIVER CLUB was a long wooden building with a string of blue lights strung around the porch. The minute you opened the door, you were greeted with the strong smell of whiskey and stale beer, and the sound of loud music and people laughing inside. Idgie loved it.

"Who Would Believe Such Pleasure . . . from a Wee Ball of Fur"

ATLANTA, GEORGIA
2015

RUTHIE WAS AT home reading the paper when the phone rang. Wondering who would be calling her so early in the morning, she picked up. It was her father, sounding extremely excited.

"Hey, Ruthie, guess what? I've got myself a cat."

"What?"

"A cat! A big long-haired orange tabby. He's sitting on the table staring at me right now."

"A real cat?"

He laughed. "Yes, a real cat."

"Who gave you a cat?"

"Nobody. I was walking around the grounds yesterday and he came strolling out of the woods, and followed me right up to my room. And when I opened the door he walked right in."

"Well, Daddy, you know he must belong to somebody."

"No. I checked. He doesn't have a collar and he's pretty beat up. So he's definitely a stray. And the poor thing was starving. He ate almost an entire chicken last night. Isn't that something?"

"Yes, but, Daddy, you know you can't have a cat at Briarwood."

"I know that. But just the same, I've got me a cat. Anyhow, honey, when you come out today, could you bring me some cat food, a kitty litter pan, and a bag of kitty litter?"

"But, Daddy, you can't have a cat."

"He's a very smart cat. I'm calling him Virgil. And by the feel of him, I'd say he's a good eighteen pounder . . . probably has a lot of coon cat in him, so be sure to pick up a lot of food."

RUTHIE HUNG UP, wondering how she was going to handle this. Her daddy couldn't have a cat. First of all, he was way too old. The thing was sure to outlive him, and then what? Second of all, it was a rule. He knew very well that Briarwood didn't allow animals. And thirdly and most important, he could trip over the thing in the middle of the night and kill himself or . . . The phone rang again. It was her father again.

"Hey, Ruthie, get me a brush, too. He's needs a good brushing, okay?"

"Daddy, listen."

"Bye, honey."

Oh God. Now what was she going to do? If she didn't buy the things he wanted, the cat would probably make a mess in his room. And, knowing him, if she didn't, he would just talk someone else into getting them. She guessed maybe the thing to do was to just humor him for a day or two and hope nobody finds out. If he was really a stray, the cat would probably run away the first chance it got.

But her main problem now was how she was going to get a kitty litter pan and a bag of kitty litter up to his room without anybody noticing.

Luckily, after a quick visit to PetSmart, she managed to slip in the side door at Briarwood carrying the two large shopping bags without being seen. She knocked on her father's door, and the moment he opened it, she hurried inside.

Bud was so glad to see her. "Oh, thank you, honey. I sure appreciate it."

She looked around. "Where's the cat?"

"He's in the bedroom napping. Wanna see him?"

She followed him and peeked inside and saw something that resembled a very large orange meatloaf lying on the bed.

"Good Lord, Daddy, that thing is the size of a mountain lion."

"I know, isn't he something? And he's the best old cat, Ruthie. All you have to do is pet him and he purrs like a kitten." Bud walked over and picked him up. "Here, hold him. He won't bite you."

"No, thank you."

As soon as Bud filled the plastic pan with kitty litter, Virgil jumped right in. He scratched around like crazy and did his cat business while Bud filled his new food dish and put it on the floor.

After Virgil finished everything in his dish and was cleaning his whiskers, Bud smiled. "Isn't he pretty, Ruthie?"

"Yes, he's very pretty. Now, Daddy, we need to talk about this."

They walked into the living room and sat down, and Virgil followed. He jumped up in Bud's lap and looked straight at her.

Bud said, "See how sweet he is, Ruthie?"

"I can see he's very sweet, Daddy, but he can't stay here. And if you really think he's a stray, I can take him over to the animal shelter in Buckhead and I'm sure they can find him a very nice home."

"He already has a nice home, and he knows it . . . don't you, boy?"

Virgil looked up at Bud and blinked at him with love in his eyes.

Ruthie could see that this cat was not going to run away anytime soon.

"Besides, I can't give him away. Don't you remember, Ruthie, when I still had my practice, people would call me and say, 'Hey, Doc, this cat or this dog just showed up at my door and won't go away, what should I do?' And I'd say, 'Well, let them in. They picked you. Animals are much smarter than we know, so you must need an animal friend, but just don't know it.'"

"But, Daddy, this is a retirement home. They have rules."

"Virgil doesn't care. I figure he's around twelve or so in cat years, as old as me. So he's ready to retire. Anyway, we had a long talk last night, and he said, 'Bud, old man, I think it's time you and me find ourselves another place to live.'"

"And what did you say?"

"I said, 'Well, Virgil, I have to agree with you. We could use a lot more room.' So I'm going to put in for a two-bedroom on the ground floor. Cats love to look out the window."

"Daddy, are you trying to get thrown out of here?"

He looked surprised. "No. We just need a little more room, don't we, boy? Oh, and one other thing. Virgil would like a scratching post and, later, when we get that extra room, one of those big cat towers."

At that moment, Virgil jumped down and sauntered over to Ruthie and rubbed against her leg.

Bud was delighted. "Aw . . . look at that, Ruthie. He likes you."

She sighed and reached down and petted him. "How big of a scratching post?"

"Oh, large to extra large should do it."

As she drove away, she wondered how in the world she was going to sneak a scratching post past Mr. Merris. Poor Daddy. He clearly loved that cat. She should have just picked Virgil up and taken him to the humane society, but her daddy looked so happy. And he really was a sweet cat. Oh dear. This was probably not going to end well.

The Eviction Notice

THE DAUGHTER WASN'T fooling anybody. Mr. Merris could clearly see on the security tape that it was a large cat scratching post she had stashed under her coat. He had suspected it. Several people had mentioned hearing a low meowing sound coming from the Threadgoode unit.

If Mr. Merris had not been so afraid of displeasing Martha Lee, he would have thrown Threadgoode out when he'd disappeared and caused such a public scene. And now this. This blatant nose-thumbing at the rules and the bylaws of Briarwood. "This will not stand. Rules are to be obeyed." Under his management, Briarwood Manor was a tight ship, and Mr. Threadgoode was rocking the boat. "Steps must be taken." He could not have the residents running amok. "Decorum must be maintained at all costs."

And if Martha Lee Caldwell did call and complain about the eviction notice, he could always blame it on the health department.

Ruthie Gets a Call

RUTHIE KNEW THIS call would be coming, she just didn't know when. But sure enough, when she answered her phone, it was Mr. Merris.

"Mrs. Caldwell, good morning. How are you this morning?"

"Why just fine, Mr. Merris. How are you?"

"Fine as well . . . thanks for asking. Uh, I'm calling because we seem to have a slight little problem."

"Oh?" she said, and waited for the shoe to drop.

"As I'm sure you know, we have a 'no animals allowed' policy here at Briarwood."

"Yes . . . I did know that."

"I see. And were you aware that your father has a live cat in his apartment?"

Ruthie didn't want to lie. She had been sneaking in food and kitty litter for over two weeks now, so she just said, "Umm . . ."

"Yes, well, anyway, he does, and unfortunately one of our cleaning ladies was unaware of that fact, as was I, and happened to open a drawer when it jumped out and attacked her. Rather severely."

"Oh no."

"So I'm sure you understand that although we hate to do it, under these circumstances, I've had to serve him an eviction notice."

"My father?"

"Oh . . . no. The cat. Now, I can let you handle the removal or one of our staff members will be happy to pick it up and take it wherever your father sees fit."

"Mr. Merris, let me talk to him first, and see what we can do."

BUD WAS WAITING for her call and started talking as soon as he picked up. "First of all, Ruthie, what was she doing opening my underwear drawer? She had no business doing that. Virgil naturally thought she was a burglar. He was just protecting my underwear."

"What was Virgil doing in your underwear drawer?"

"He sleeps there. It's his daytime nap place."

"Mr. Merris said the cat attacked her."

"Oh, for God's sake. I saw it. It was nothing. He barely broke the skin. The woman is just trying to make a big deal out of it."

"Well, whatever, but Mr. Merris told me he's sent an eviction notice. What are you going to do?"

"I don't know yet."

"Well, should I come and get the cat?"

"No. . . . Oh, I don't know. I'll call you back."

After she hung up she felt so bad. Poor Daddy, he seemed so upset. She guessed she could always bring Virgil home with her, but that might cause another big problem. Martha Lee was deathly allergic to animal hair, so she would never be able to come over to the house anymore.

The more Ruthie thought about it, the more she realized that might not be a bad idea.

The Insurrection

THE NEXT AFTERNOON when they came back from lunch, all the residents at Briarwood Manor found a bulletin that had been shoved under their door.

ATTENTION ALL RESIDENTS
Please attend town hall meeting in auditorium
tonight at 8:00.
VERY IMPORTANT!!

Everyone was curious and wondered what it was about. That night after dinner, they all filed in to the auditorium and were surprised to see Bud Threadgoode up on the stage, sitting beside a small table. On the table was what looked to be an animal carrier. Some of the people seated up front saw that there was something orange inside, moving around.

Everyone was seated. Including Mr. Merris, who had been reached at home and informed about the impromptu meeting. Bud stood up.

"Good evening, ladies and gentleman. Thank you so much for coming. I'm sure you are wondering why I called this meeting tonight. It is to discuss the serious matter of Mr. Virgil vs. Briarwood Manor, Inc."

He tapped on the carrier and said, "Mr. Virgil has chosen me to speak on his behalf, due to the fact that although he understands English, he does not speak it. So let me get straight to the point. Two days ago, Mr. Virgil was sent an eviction notice and was ordered to vacate the premises within three days. The notice cited an infraction of rule number 246 in the Briarwood Manor bylaws. An infraction that Mr. Virgil is vigorously protesting on the grounds that, number one, possession is nine-tenths of the law, and number two, that he is probably the quietest resident here, and also the cleanest. He does not smoke, drink, or entertain members of the opposite sex in his room, nor does he throw any wild parties. In fact, if anything, he believes his presence has improved Briarwood Manor by eliminating three large rodents from the premises, and he is willing to place what is left of said rats in evidence." Bud held up a small sack and put it back down.

"Mr. Virgil and I would like the opportunity to challenge rule 246 established in 1947, which states, 'Residents may not under any circumstances feed or keep any animal on premises,' on grounds that this rule is outdated and inhumane.

"This same law restricts residents from keeping even a tiny little songbird. Mr. Virgil and I further contend that of all the age groups, seniors in particular need something alive around them. Something they can love and care for. And with so many little homeless animals needing homes, we believe that changing this rule would be beneficial for all parties.

"Now, as shareholders in Briarwood Manor, Inc., we as residents have the majority of votes to overturn laws as we see fit. So let me put it to a vote. How many would not object to a neighbor keeping a small animal, and if you could, would any of you be interested in having a kitten?" Bud looked out across the room, and several hands went up at once. One by one, many others slowly followed.

Bud looked out. "Good. Okay, then let's discuss the possibilities of . . ."

But before Bud could continue his speech, a lady in the third row stood up and said, "Hey, Bud, how about rabbits? They don't bark and they can be housetrained."

Several people in the audience nodded and murmured in agreement.

Another man in the back shouted out, "What about ferrets? I love ferrets."

Mr. Merris moaned and sank down lower and lower in his seat. When the meeting ended and people lined up to come up onstage and pet Virgil, he could see the handwriting on the wall. And two days later, after the official vote was taken and sent to the board, his goose was cooked.

When Bud heard the news, he looked over at Virgil, who was curled up on his new KittyTower sound asleep. "Well, Virgil, you've scored a big victory, and you don't even know it."

Within the first six months, five baby kittens and three senior cats found permanent homes at Briarwood, and a lot of the residents were now working with the local ASPCA, fostering kittens and bunnies, one ferret, and one baby owl until they could find good homes for them.

And it was so pleasant to walk down the halls and hear the cheerful little bird tweets coming from the rooms. Even Mr. Merris had to admit there was a lot more happy chatter at the dinner table every night. The residents had a lot of fun showing each other photos of their pets and swapping stories about all the cute and funny things they'd done that day.

And even Mr. Merris started bringing his little dachshund Winnie to work with him.

. . .

A MONTH LATER, Bud was moved into a larger apartment on the ground floor with a nice window for Virgil. Later he said, "You know, Ruthie, whenever I come back to my place and see those two orange ears in the window waiting for me, it just means the world to me."

The Will

RUTHIE WAS FLIPPING through one of her old *Veranda* magazines and wishing she had the money to redo her living room when her father called.

"Hey, honey."

"Hi. What are you up to today?"

"Well, I'm making a few little changes to my will, and I need to talk to you about something."

"Oh, Daddy, I don't want to talk about wills. You know it upsets me."

"I know, honey, but here's the thing. Now, I'm not saying that it will, but if anything should happen to me, I need to make arrangements for Virgil."

"Oh."

"And my question to you is, would it upset you terribly if Lois took him? She knows I'm doing my will, and she asked me if she could have him. She lives across the hall and she just loves him. But now, if you want him, I'll just tell her that I'm leaving him to my daughter."

"No, no. That's all right, Daddy. Listen, if she wants him, let her have him."

"Well, I'm glad, Ruthie. I think he'd be happier staying here, in a place he's used to. And he likes Lois. So good. She'll be glad to hear it."

"Was that all?"

"No. There's something else. Do you remember that surprise I told you that you were getting when I died?"

"Yes?"

"Well, I have decided not to wait. I'm giving it to you now."

"Oh my gosh, what is it?"

"Are you ready?"

"Yes."

"It's your mother's frog collection. I know you probably thought we gave them away when we moved, but I saved them for you. There are over two hundred of them. I had them in storage, and I'm having them sent over to you. So what do you think? Are you surprised?"

"Speechless."

WHEN SHE HUNG up, Ruthie felt a slight sense of relief. If anything ever happened to Daddy, of course, she would have taken Virgil. But it sounded like he would be better off with Lois. Then she wondered, who was Lois? And how did she know Daddy was doing his will? Of course, Daddy giving her the inheritance now was a sweet thought. But looking around the room, she wondered what in God's name was she going to do with two hundred frog figurines.

Evelyn's Call

ATLANTA, GEORGIA
December 2015

RUTHIE GOT IN the car and immediately wiped her hands with the disinfectant gel she kept in the glove compartment. She looked at her hair in the rear-view mirror and sighed. Just as she had thought. One side of her hair was definitely shorter than the other. Not only had Mimi given her a terrible haircut, she had probably given her the flu as well. And right before Christmas, too. Of course, Mimi hadn't told Ruthie she was sick until her head was in the bowl and her hair was soaking wet and covered in shampoo. It was only after Mimi started coughing that she said, "Sorry. I've got the flu, but I came in anyway. I hate to disappoint my customers." Ruthie had spent the next hour trying not to breathe.

Later, as she pulled into her driveway, she waved at Martha Lee's small army of gardeners who were busy stringing Christmas lights and raking leaves.

When she walked into the house, she saw that her message light was blinking and pushed the button. It was her daughter Carolyn, telling her how sorry she was, but she was not going to make it home to Atlanta for Christmas. She didn't say why. But it really didn't matter. The point was that Ruthie and her dad would be spending another Christmas alone. Ruthie had spent Thanksgiving at Carolyn's house in Washington last year. But anytime she tried to help, cook, or even wash the dishes, Carolyn would stop her. "No, Mother, don't do that. You just go sit in the living room and enjoy yourself."

Her son, Richard, was a different story. His lack of enthusiasm for a career in business had been somewhat of a disappointment to Brooks, because he'd hoped that one day Richard would join the family business. But Richard had chosen a different route in life. He and his girlfriend, Dotsie, were now living off the grid in a small town in southern Oregon. Both were vegan and avid bicyclists who grew their own kale.

Last summer, when Ruthie had visited them on their small farm, she'd almost starved to death. She dearly loved her son, and Dotsie was very sweet, but kale just wasn't her thing. By the end of the week, she would have killed for a cheeseburger.

But Richard and Dotsie seemed extremely happy. And Carolyn, who lived in the very thick of Washington's social world, was not just happy, but deliriously happy. For different reasons, both of her children were doing just fine. Ruthie seemed to be the only one floundering at the moment.

Lately she had begun to wonder whether this feeling of uselessness she had, had nothing to do with them. Maybe it was that she needed to get out and do something other than sit in the same house, on the same Circle, in the same rut for the rest of her life. Dear God, from where she started out in life, full of hope and ambition, how in the world did she wind up here? She went upstairs and got into bed, waiting for the flu to hit.

A FEW HOURS later, just as Ruthie was about to get up from her nap, the phone rang. It was Evelyn Couch calling from Birmingham.

"Hey. What are you doing?"

"I'm in bed with a bad haircut. How about you?"

"I'm bored."

"Oh God, me too. I'm so bored, I'm even boring myself."

"Hey, Ruthie, I've been thinking. You're bored. I'm bored. So, you wanna have a little fun?"

"Sure. As long as it's legal."

Evelyn laughed. "It is. How about you coming over to Birmingham this weekend? I have a little something I want to run by you."

"I'll be happy to come, but don't look at my hair."

"I promise. Text me when you have an ETA."

Evelyn's call couldn't have come at a better time. Now that she had something to look forward to, Ruthie felt much better. And they always had a good time together.

Ruthie wondered if what she wanted to run by her was the possibility of the two of them taking another trip. Evelyn had planned the last one. In May they'd gone on a cruise to Hawaii together and had a ball. They had even taken hula lessons on the ship. Ruthie had to admit that although Evelyn was older, she could sure swing those hips. When she told Evelyn that, Evelyn laughed and said, "Well, honey, I've got a lot more hips to swing."

It had been so good to get away from the Circle and Martha Lee for just a little while. One night, when they were at poolside on the ship enjoying their piña coladas, Ruthie suddenly realized something and turned to Evelyn. "You know, Evelyn, you're my Ninny Threadgoode."

"What do you mean?"

"Well, I was feeling so down, then you called and here I am, sailing on the deep blue sea without a care in the world."

Evelyn said, "And if it hadn't been for Ninny, I would never have met you or your father. Or Virgil."

Evelyn picked up her piña colada and held it up. "Let's drink to Ninny Threadgoode."

Ruthie joined her, "Hear! Hear! To Ninny Threadgoode. Wherever you are!"

Just then, the Hawaiian orchestra started playing "Lovely Hula Hands" and Evelyn turned to Ruth. "Wanna do it?"

"Oh, why not. You only live once, right?"

"Right, and if you're lucky, twice!"

Once they were out on the dance floor doing the hula steps they had just learned, a man named Morrie at the next table whispered to his wife. "Irma, look at those two gals go. That heavyset one sure can move."

Time Ran Out

KISSIMMEE, FLORIDA
1989

IDGIE HAD ALWAYS threatened to come up to Maryland and visit Bud and Peggy, but she never had. After Julian died, she was left to manage his orange groves and run her fruit and honey stand alone.

And then, too, she had been busy tending to official duties. After many years of her holding court at the fruit stand, everybody in town had started calling Idgie "The Mayor," and ten years later, darned if they didn't officially elect her as the first female mayor of Kissimmee. At the time they'd made a big deal out of it, and *The Miami Herald* sent a reporter to interview her. But Idgie, being Idgie, had her photo taken alongside two of Julian's old nanny goats, telling the reporter that they were senior members of her city council.

DURING THOSE YEARS, Bud and Peggy had planned to get back down to visit her, too, but they had been so busy running the clinic together and raising Ruthie that they had not made it. Bud would never forgive himself for that. Idgie had raised him, paid for his college, and encouraged him all his life. He and Peggy had planned to retire in Florida, and buy a house next to Idgie. It would be so much fun. They could go fishing, and bang around in the woods just like the old days. But that had never happened.

Idgie hadn't told them how ill she was, or they would have moved heaven and earth to get down there sooner. They thought they had all the time in the world. So had Idgie. She never did slow down, but finally, after she got so weak she couldn't do things for herself, she moved to a local nursing facility. Every day, up until the last few days, her room was filled with visitors and AA friends.

When the doctor told Helen, a hospice nurse who had been taking care of Idgie, that it was time to call in the relatives, it was sad news. Helen had grown so fond of Idgie these past weeks. So after having a good little cry in the bathroom, she pulled herself together and went into Idgie's room.

Idgie smiled at her weakly and said, "Good morning, sunshine."

Helen started moving some of the flower arrangements around, and casually said, "Honey, the doctor thinks it might be a good idea if we call Bud, and just let him know you're here."

Idgie looked alarmed and struggled to sit up. "Oh, Helen, no. Promise me you won't call Buddy."

"Well, sweetie, don't you think he should know?"

"No. That boy is busy and he doesn't need to run all the way down here. It'll be too upsetting for him to see me lookin' like an old bag of bones. Promise me you won't call him."

"Well . . . if that's what you want."

"It is. And, besides, I'm ready to go on to a better place, as they say." Then she winked at Helen. "Unless, of course, I go straight to hell. But that wouldn't bother me. Hell couldn't be any hotter than Florida in August."

. . .

THEY SAID SHE had a peaceful ending. When Helen called Bud and let him know, she explained to him why she had not called him sooner. He was sad to hear it, but he understood. Idgie knew it would have been too hard on both of them. Besides, in her will, she had named Bud as her sole heir, so there could be no guessing on his part about how she felt about him. It had been easier for her to say goodbye that way. Idgie hadn't wanted a service of any kind. All she wanted was to be taken back to Whistle Stop and buried next to Ruth and the rest of her family. And she was.

Imogene "Idgie" Threadgoode
1908–1989
HAPPY TO BE HOME

The New Proposition

RUTHIE ARRIVED AT Evelyn's house just in time for lunch, and after they had caught up on all the news, Ruthie said, "I'm curious, what was the idea you want to run by me?"

Evelyn smiled. "It's just a little something I've been thinking about."

"What?"

"About the two of us and our situations. I'm a widow, and you're a widow."

"Sad but true."

"So, do you think you'll ever get married again, Ruthie?"

"I don't think so. I could never find a man to take Brooks's place. He was the one and only for me. But what about you?"

"Definitely not. I like being single. Besides, all the men my age want young chicks, or else they want somebody to take care of them."

"That's true."

"So, Ruthie, what are we going to do with the rest of our lives?"

Ruthie looked at her and said, "Funny you should ask. I have absolutely no idea."

"Well, funny enough I do. Finish your tea and get in the car."

. . .

As they were driving, Evelyn had a big smile on her face, and that piqued Ruthie's curiosity even more. She still didn't know enough about Birmingham to know where they were going, but as far as she could tell, they seemed to be driving out of town and then circling around.

"Where are you taking me? Back to Georgia?"

"You'll see . . . soon enough."

Evelyn followed the voice on her GPS and made a left turn and drove down a long, one-lane gravel road and pulled up to a spot by some railroad tracks and stopped the car. "Here we are."

Ruthie looked around. There was nothing much to see but junk and a bunch of old vine-covered buildings. "I guessed that, but where is here?"

"Hop out and I'll show you." Ruthie got out and Evelyn said, "Welcome to Whistle Stop."

"What? You're kidding. This . . . is Whistle Stop? Oh my gosh. Are you sure?"

"Yes, I'm sure. I just bought it."

"What?"

"I own it!"

Ruthie looked around at the piles of junk and weeds everywhere. "But why would you buy it?"

"Well . . . you're looking for something to do, and so am I. So, let's you and me open up the old Whistle Stop Cafe again. And maybe even the whole town. Wouldn't Bud love that?"

"Of course," said Ruthie. "He would be thrilled, but how can we do it? I mean, look, it's all falling down."

"Easy. I had my guys look into it, and they can get some of the original building plans from the county planning office. We save what buildings we can, and then rebuild what we can't, following the old plans."

"Really?"

"Yes. So what do you say? It'll be a lot of fun. I know it's a big project, but we can do it."

"But, Evelyn, won't it cost a lot of money to do something like that?"

Evelyn waved it off. "Oh, honey, I've got lots of money to invest, and I'd rather do this than have it sit in a bank."

"Really?"

"Oh yes. And with your talent for decorating, we could make this place look just like it used to, only better."

"Do you think we could?"

"Absolutely. Right now, it's out in the middle of nowhere, but after we put in all new roads in and out, I think people will come in droves. In a few years, we could have a whole new town, with houses and condos."

Ruthie looked at her friend with awe. "Evelyn, you never cease to amaze me."

"Of course this means you would have to move to Birmingham," Evelyn said, "for at least for a year. Will you do it?"

"Of course I will."

And so the "Revitalize Whistle Stop" project began.

THE NEXT MORNING, as they were going over to discuss plans with Evelyn's contractor, Ruthie was getting even more excited about the project.

She said, "Oh, Evelyn, to be able to do this for Daddy. He wanted to come back home so badly, even though it wasn't there anymore. He almost killed himself just to see where it used to be. Just imagine how happy he'll be when he sees the cafe, and maybe the town, all put back together again."

Evelyn said, "He's going to be very surprised."

Ruthie sighed with relief. "I've wanted so much to do something nice for him. He's at an age when I could lose him for good. Now, thanks to you, I *can* do something. And I can't think of a better present to give him than this."

"Agreed," Evelyn said. "But let's don't let him see it until we get it all cleaned up first. Then we can show it to him and surprise him."

Only in America

ONLY IN AMERICA could a girl who had started out in the world with not much of anything end up becoming a multimillionaire. One whose only job was to figure out a way to spend her money on good, solid investments. Evelyn had found that, with the way Birmingham was growing, any commercial property close by would always be a good safe investment. Over the years, she had bought raw parcels of land that had been developed into shopping malls and office parks.

Three weeks ago, Ted Campbell, her realtor, had called and said he'd found a thirty-acre parcel outside of town that Evelyn might want to take a look at. Ted knew she always liked a property with a long view and lots of open land.

The next morning, standing with Ted and looking down the railroad tracks, she felt she could see for miles. She loved it. Not only did she love it, the moment they started driving down the road along the tracks, Evelyn realized she'd been to this place before. She told Ted to go ahead and write up an offer.

Ninny Threadgoode had always talked about Whistle Stop with so much affection. She knew it would have pleased Ninny so much to know that she was buying it. And the price was certainly right, if you considered that she was purchasing an entire little town, including the cemetery and some of the buildings that were still standing. Good heavens, at that asking price, she couldn't afford not to buy it!

Telling Daddy

ATLANTA, GEORGIA

THE VERY FIRST thing Ruthie did after she got back to Atlanta was call her father and ask him out to lunch at his favorite place.

As he was polishing off his second helping of black-eyed peas, she said, "Daddy, would you mind terribly if I move over to Birmingham, at least for a while?

He seemed surprised. "Birmingham?"

"Yes. Here's the thing. Evelyn has a project she wants to do, and she's asked me to be her partner on it. But it would mean my being gone quite a bit."

"Oh?"

"I could still come over every week to see you, and I thought that now that you have Virgil and your new friend, Lucy—"

"Lois."

"Lois, that's right. I thought you might not mind. And, remember, I won't be that far away, and . . ."

Bud stopped her. "Honey, if that's what you want to do, you go right ahead. Don't worry about me. I'm just fine with it. And you know I think the world of Evelyn. What kind of a project is it?"

"It's just a little building development she's working on. I'll tell you more about it later. So, great then. I'll be staying in Evelyn's guest cottage. Okay?"

"Of course it's okay. I'm tickled pink for you, honey, I really am. I didn't want to say anything before, but I don't think you've been very happy lately, and a change of scenery might cheer you up."

"I think so. And I think it will be fun."

"Well, this is good news. Hey, let's celebrate your new project. How about we have a piece of that lemon icebox pie?"

"Let's do."

"And maybe some coconut cake?"

"Oh, why not?"

Later, when Ruthie drove him back to Briarwood, she walked in with him and Bud said, "Hey, Ruthie, would you like to meet my friend Lois? I know she wants to meet you."

"Well, sure, if you want me to."

"You wait here and I'll run get her."

A few minutes later he came back with Lois. Ruthie was surprised to see that Lois, as it turned out, was a lovely older lady, impeccably dressed in a stylish outfit and wearing the most beautiful string of pearls Ruthie had ever seen. Not to mention the diamond ring she had on that was the size of a small doorknob.

"Oh, Ruthie," Lois said. "May I call you Ruthie? I've heard so much about you, and I'm just delighted to meet you at long last."

WHEN RUTHIE GOT home and thought about her upcoming move to Birmingham, she realized that a project this big could take more than a year, maybe two. There was really no point in keeping the house in Atlanta just sitting there empty and costing her money every month. Money that would only sink her deeper into debt. And the house really was too big for just one person anyway. Maybe this was the right time to finally sell it and find a small apartment to rent somewhere close to her father for when she visited. It would mean taking a big chance and putting all her eggs and her future into one basket. But she felt if she didn't do it now, she never would. She would close her eyes and take the leap. "Look out, Whistle Stop, here I come."

WHEN SHE TOLD her children about the plan, her son, Richard, thought it all sounded great, but Carolyn was having an absolute flying fit over it. For days, there were hysterical phone calls from Washington.

"That's our family home, Mother. You can't just sell it. And where will I stay when I come to Atlanta?"

"Well, honey, you can stay at your grandmother's, as you always do."

"But I want to be able to come across the Circle and visit you. And why are you going to Alabama for a year? Who will look after Granddaddy?"

"He's just fine at Briarwood, and Birmingham is not that far away. If anything happened I could be home in a couple of hours."

"But I don't want strangers living in my home."

"I am using your grandmother's agent, and she will make sure they won't be strangers. She's already said her friends from the club, the Vaughans, are interested in buying it. I'm sure you know them."

"Well, all I can say, Mother, is that if Daddy were still alive, he would be very upset."

Actually, knowing Brooks, he would have been very happy that she was moving forward with her life.

Let the Project Begin!

BY THE TIME Ruthie got back to Atlanta, Evelyn had already se-
cured her financing, had a set of building plans drawn up, and
hired a cleaning crew that was ready to go. The first thing they
had to do was clear out all the junk around the area, then chop
down the vines and inspect the buildings underneath. And it was
amazing what they found. Opal Butts's beauty shop was pretty
much intact, even the old hair dryers were still standing, and,
stacked on the shelves, there were still some bottles of shampoo
and old unused hair dye.

Sadly, the cafe had been pretty well emptied out. The counter
and the wooden booths were still there, along with a few tables
and chairs, but that was about it. But to Ruthie and Evelyn's relief,
some of the buildings on the block did not seem to have too much
structural damage.

During the first week the cleanup crew uncovered an old
wooden storage shed in the back of the cafe. Ruthie and Evelyn
drove over to the site to inspect the contents. Inside were the cafe's
original screen door, with the words FRIED GREEN TOMATOES written on it, an old stand-up piano, and a very large deer head. And
stacked in a corner were boxes and boxes of Christmas ornaments,
and one Santa Claus suit in moth balls. They also found packs of
unopened Juicy Fruit gum and Red Man chewing tobacco, a
1930 calendar, and an empty cigar box.

But for Ruthie, the best of all the treasures they discovered that day were about twenty framed photos that someone had wrapped in a blanket. One was a picture of Idgie and Ruth and little Buddy standing in front of the cafe. Bud looked to be around five at the time and was wearing a sun suit and little white leather sandals. And there were lots of photos of Sipsey and Big George. Evelyn was delighted to see a picture of Ninny and her husband, Cleo, posing with Julian and Idgie. It was a happy trip back in time. The last picture they unwrapped was a photo of a ventriloquist dummy, signed "To Buddy, Love Chester."

"Who's Chester?" asked Evelyn.

"I haven't a clue."

"Me, neither, but as soon as the cafe is finished, all of these are going back up on the walls exactly where they were. Won't that be great?"

Ruthie was just thrilled with what they had found. Her plan was to make the cafe look as authentic as possible, and she could use everything—the deer head, the piano, the Christmas ornaments, and maybe even the old Santa Claus suit.

By the time the cleanup crew had finished, they had removed around five tons of old cars, trucks, and piles of junk. After it was all cleared out, the area started to look much better.

A few weeks later, the entire block and all the remaining houses were tented for termites. All of the construction work, including the new paved roads and new sewer lines, was set to begin as soon as the building permits came through, which their contractor said should be any day now.

So, while they were waiting to start the work, Ruthie thought it would be the perfect time to bring her daddy over and show him what they were planning. She had hoped the cleanup would be finished by his birthday, and it was. She couldn't wait to surprise him.

23 and Who?

BACK AT CALDWELL Circle, Martha Lee felt as though a very large brick wall had suddenly fallen on top of her. She had just received the most devastating news of her life. At the moment, she was in a dark room, stretched out on the divan, barely able to move from the sheer impact of it. From this day forward, her life, as she knew it, was over. How could she go on? What would be the point? As she lay there listening to her heart still pounding from the shock, she wondered if she had the courage to kill herself.

Not more than thirty minutes ago, she had received the final results from her 23andMe DNA test, which had revealed she was 70 percent English, 2 percent Irish, and 28 percent Chinese. Gerta, her social secretary, had done more research and discovered that, unfortunately, Martha's male Lee ancestor had not been Duke Edmond James Lee, but a Chinese horticulturist named Henry Wong Lee, who had been hired to oversee the family estate. The portrait hanging in the living room, the one she had shown to all Atlanta, was of a woman she was not even related to.

After Martha read the results, she was so weak she was barely able to reach over and ring the small silver bell on the end table. As soon as Gerta heard the faint ding-ding of the bell, she hurried across the hall to the library. When she opened the door and saw Martha Lee's ashen face, she was alarmed.

"Mrs. Caldwell, are you all right?"

Martha Lee looked over and said wistfully, "No, dear. I'll never be all right again, as long as I live. Tell Cook to bring me a large glass of cold gin and a gun."

"A gun? Oh, Mrs. Caldwell, I can't do that. I'd be afraid to even pick up a gun. I just couldn't. Why, you might hurt yourself."

Martha sighed. "Oh, all right, then. Just bring the gin."

SOMEHOW, MARTHA LEE survived the next few weeks without doing herself in. And today she even had a small glimmer of hope that maybe all was not lost after all. Gerta was now extremely busy tracing the history of all the Chinese dynasties, desperately looking for a connection with the Wong or Lee family to one of the ancient Manchu emperors. And, as she told Martha Lee, who knows? She might be able to find a direct line straight back to the Dowager Empress herself.

After Martha Lee had some time to calm down a bit, she realized this new revelation about her ancestry actually made some sense. She had always been partial to all things Far Eastern: art, rugs, furniture. And she did have the largest collection of Ming vases in Atlanta. And Dowager Empress . . . oh, she liked the sound of that.

And as she told Gerta, "One must follow one's genes, don't you think?"

Gerta agreed. She was 98 percent German, and she had loved beer all her life.

. . .

A MONTH LATER, just when Martha Lee was getting her spirits back, she was struck another blow. Her late husband's lawyer, who handled all their financial affairs, came to the house and informed her that she was running out of money, and could no longer afford to keep her home. She was not happy to hear this.

"How long do I have before I will be forced to leave?"

"Six months at least." He looked around the room, and said, "Of course, you could buy yourself a little more time here, Martha."

"How?"

"You could sell some of your antiques. You have quite a collection. I imagine those vases could bring in a good amount."

Martha Lee was indignant. "What? I couldn't possibly sell my collection. These are not just antiques, Ronald." Martha Lee waved her arm in the direction of the vases. "These are precious family heirlooms that go back in my family for over six centuries."

"I see. Well then, Martha, you might want to start looking into Briarwood."

The Surprise

Bud picked up the phone and it was Ruthie.

"Hey, Daddy, how are you?"

"Well, hello there. Where are you?"

"Still in Birmingham."

"Ah . . . still working away on your project?"

"Oh, yes. But I know someone who is having a birthday this Sunday."

"Don't remind me. I'm trying to forget it."

"Listen, Daddy, do you think maybe your friend Lois could look after Mr. Virgil for a few days?"

"I'm sure she would, why?"

"Because I want you to come over to Birmingham for your birthday; I have something I want to show you. What if I pick you up at Briarwood Saturday morning, and then bring you back Monday morning? Will you do it?"

"Sure, sounds like fun."

Saturday afternoon, after she and Bud arrived at Evelyn's house and had visited a bit, Ruthie said, "Daddy, Evelyn and I have a surprise for you. We want to take you somewhere, but you have to promise to do exactly what we say."

"Okay," he said.

When they got to Evelyn's car, Ruthie said, "Get in and don't ask any questions."

He laughed and got in and sat down.

"Now, Daddy, I'm going to tie this handkerchief over your eyes and you are not to take it off until we tell you to."

"Am I being kidnapped?"

"Yes."

He giggled. "Y'all are not driving me to the loony bin, are you?"

"No. You just behave, and you'll see soon enough."

As THEY DROVE around Gate City and down the old one-lane gravel road, Ruthie was afraid he might guess where he was, but he didn't.

Evelyn pulled up and parked right across the street from the cafe.

"Are we here?" Bud asked.

"Yes, but don't you look until I tell you." They both got out and helped him out of the car, then turned him around and faced him toward the cafe. Ruthie said, "Okay. You can look now."

Bud smiled and pulled off the handkerchief and for a moment, he seemed to not know where he was.

"Daddy, it's Whistle Stop! Look, there's the old cafe and the beauty shop."

Bud was clearly stunned. "I see it, but I can't believe it. I thought it was all gone! They told me there was nothing left out here but a pile of junk."

Evelyn said, "There wasn't, but Ruthie and I had it all cleaned up, and we are going to rebuild the entire town from the ground up."

"You're kidding."

"No, Daddy, a lot of it is still here. It just needs to be rebuilt."

"You have got to be kidding. Is this the project you gals have been working on?"

"Yes, Evelyn bought the entire town. And we are going to re-open the old cafe, and hopefully bring in more businesses. What do you think?"

"I can't think. I'm still in a state of shock." He looked at Evelyn. "You bought the whole town?"

"Well, Bud, I figured that the way Birmingham is spreading out so fast, as soon as we get our roads built and have access to the interstate, it's going to change everything. I believe we can get people to start moving out here again."

"You do?"

"Sure. We'll start with a few little housing developments, and with the right kind of advertising, I don't think we can miss."

When they went inside the old cafe building, Bud stood there for a moment and looked around. "My God, I haven't been in this room for over sixty-something years. I can't believe we're both still standing."

Ruthie said, "I was looking for something to do, so after it's all been redone, I'm going to move into the back room, and manage it."

Ruthie then told him how she planned to re-create the exterior and interior of the cafe, just as it had been in the 1930s. "People love that sort of old-time campy look."

Bud said, "I can help you there, Ruthie. I can remember exactly where everything was. The old piano was right over in the corner. And a deer head was right up there."

Evelyn laughed. "Well Ruthie, it looks like you have your creative assistant."

Before they left the cafe, they showed Bud all the old photos they had found. He looked at them one by one and said, "Oh my God, there's little Chester, I haven't thought about him in years."

"What we want to know is, who was little Chester?"

Bud laughed. "Just a friend of mine. We used to be pen pals."

Ruthie shook her head. "Only you, Daddy, would have a dummy for a pen pal."

They made a stop at the cemetery to visit Idgie's, Ruth's, and Ninny's graves. Then later they walked him around the area, and showed him all the different houses they were planning to restore. The last house they showed him was in pretty bad disrepair and all the paint was gone, but when Bud saw it he said, "Oh my gosh. This is Aunt Ninny and Uncle Cleo's old house. Oh my gosh. I spent many an hour over here. Aunt Ninny used to read the funny papers to us kids, right up there on the porch."

They headed up the steps to the front door, and Ruthie said, "Daddy, wait. Before we go inside, I have something I want you to have." She handed him the key to the front door and said, "Happy Birthday, Daddy, from both of us."

Bud stared at the key and then looked back at Ruthie. "I don't understand."

"The house is yours. It's your birthday present."

"You don't mean it." He looked at Evelyn.

Evelyn said, "Yes, she does. And we are going to fix it up just for you . . . and Virgil, of course."

Bud was astounded. "You mean, I don't have to stay at Briarwood anymore?"

"No, Daddy. This is your home, if you want it. What do you say?"

"Well, I just don't know *what* to say. You gals are about to give me a heart attack."

Evelyn said, "You'd better say yes. Will you come?"

"Will I? When can I move in?"

"Just as soon as we can get it finished," said Evelyn.

"I still can't believe it. Ruthie, when can I tell Merris I'm leaving?"

"We don't have a firm date yet, but we'll have them work as fast as they can."

"Oh my, I never thought I'd see Whistle Stop again. And now I'm gonna be living here."

His eyes suddenly filled with tears. "Ruthie, Evelyn, I guess this is about the best present I ever got."

RUTHIE KNEW IT was going to be a lot of hard work getting everything done, but seeing her father's face light up as it had when he saw Whistle Stop again would make it all worth it. Although Bud never said so, she realized from his reaction today just how unhappy he had been living at Briarwood. She hadn't seen him so excited about something in a long time. Thank heavens she was going to be able to get him out and bring him back home where he belonged. She wanted his last years to be happy ones.

Over the next few weeks Evelyn and Ruthie were having a lot of fun with the plans to redo Ninny's old house for Bud. It was going to be the same as it had been, except now it would have a brand-new walk-in tub and shower, and be wheelchair accessible, just in case he needed it at some time in the future. The architect also drew up plans for a small apartment in the back for a caregiver, in case the time came when he might need one. Bud was calling almost every day from Atlanta, wanting to know how everything was coming along. Ruthie was excited and champing at the bit to start, and get him moved into his new house. But then something unexpected happened.

Bud might not be moving home after all.

Very Bad News

IT HAD TAKEN a while, but by now almost all of the building permits had been pulled and the project was finally getting ready to move ahead full steam. Today, they were preparing to start the restoration of the cafe. The crew was up in the attic, checking for any structural damage they might need to shore up before they began, busy examining all the wooden rafters with flashlights, when the contractor in charge walked in and called them down. "Pack up your tools, boys, and go on home. You're done for the day."

JIM CARDER, THE owner of the road construction company Evelyn and Ruthie had hired, was still waiting for his permits to start work. He'd finally gone over to the Jefferson County Courthouse to see if he could find out what the big holdup was. When he got there, the man in charge of all sewer and roadway easements sat him down in his office with a map and told him the bad news.

"Jim, these roads and sewer lines you are proposing run directly through private property. I'm sorry, but I can't give you your permit to build."

"What? Doesn't Mrs. Couch own that land?"

"Most of it, yes. But right here," he pointed to a section on the map between Evelyn's property and the interstate, "there's this twenty-acre parcel that belongs to another party, and it's through here that your utilities need to be accessed."

"Well, not only that," said Jim, "the whole project depends on us getting access to the interstate off-ramp. She's planning to put a whole new development and businesses out there. Without that access, we are landlocked. We have to get a right-of-way."

"I understand that, Jim, so all I can do is give you a copy of the deed, and maybe you can work something out with the owner. Maybe they'll sell it, or grant you an easement. But until then, my hands are tied. I'm sorry."

"Oh, man. Evelyn's already spent a fortune cleaning up the place, drawing up plans. Why in the hell didn't you tell me this sooner?"

"We didn't know it ourselves until just a few days ago. My assistant pulled out an old map, looking for the location of the original sewer lines, and saw a different name on the parcel. I sent him up to the hall of records to have them check and see if it was some kind of mistake. It took a while for them to get back to us, but it wasn't a mistake. They have it on file that that particular parcel had been transferred out of the Johnson family land, on November 3, 1932, and signed over to a Mr. Arvel Ligget of Pell City, Alabama. Here's a copy of the deed transfer."

Jim took it and looked at it. "Is this thing legal?"

"I'm afraid so. It was notarized, signed, and witnessed by a Miss Eva Bates."

"Who in the hell is Arvel Ligget? Nineteen thirty-two? Hell, he's gotta be long dead by now."

. . .

AFTER THREE WEEKS of digging up old records, they found that Arvel Ligget was, in fact, long dead, and had died without a will. However, he had forty-two relatives who for years now had been fighting one another, tooth and nail, over all his land holdings, including the twenty acres near Whistle Stop, each claiming to be the rightful heir. There was nobody they could buy it from, or even try to negotiate an easement with.

When Jim broke the news to Evelyn and Ruthie, they were both devastated. Jim told them the only thing they could do now was delay the project and try to wait it out, but he wasn't hopeful. With so many lawsuits pending, getting a final ruling on the legal ownership of the land could take years. And even then, they didn't know whether the declared owner would be willing to strike a deal with them.

Evelyn knew that without access to the interstate, continuing with the project would just be throwing good money after bad. And so, after she talked it over with Ruthie, the project was shut down.

She said, "I'm so sorry, Ruthie. . . . Blame me. I'm the one who drug you into this mess."

"Don't be silly, Evelyn. It's not your fault."

"But still, I feel terrible, after you've just sold your house. . . . Of course, I can see about other projects we can try and do. . . ."

"Oh, I know. . . . It's really Daddy that I'm most concerned about. He's been so excited, thinking he was going to move back home. I'm afraid this is going to break his heart. And to tell the truth, I guess I am disappointed for myself. I know it may sound silly, but being over here, hearing so many stories about her, I don't know why, but I sort of felt that Aunt Idgie might have been passing the baton on to me, and that I might be the new Idgie Threadgoode. Maybe carry on her legacy somehow."

Evelyn said, "I understand."

"I met her once down in Florida when I was a little girl."

"You did? You never told me that."

"It was so long ago, I barely remember it. I was just a kid. But I do remember that I really liked her. I remember that."

Dot Weems

Dear Folks,

I'm sure by now you all know that I lost Wilbur in June. I am grateful for all the years we did have, but sometimes it sure hurts to be a human being. I know I am not alone. So many of us have lost our loved ones. The price we pay for living a long life, I guess. And it's not just losing the person, it's losing the person you have shared so many special memories with, and you realize that they are just your memories now. That's why it's doubly important that we don't lose touch. My old Whistle Stop gang are now the only ones I have left whom I can ask, "Do you remember when . . . ?" I've often wondered where all those memories go after we die. Are they still floating around up in the ether somewhere, or do they die with us? If so, just think of all the billions of lovely memories that just fade and die away.

Anyway, it's going to be a gloomy old Christmas without my Wilbur. So I hope you all will understand and forgive me if I don't do the long Christmas letter this year.

Sending my love to all,

Dot

Dot Weems

A short update:

Hey, gang, just when I decided to not care about Christmas at all this year, something wonderful happened. First, I have to backtrack to a day last summer. Wilbur and I went to the jewelry store to buy a new crystal for his old railroad pocket watch. And while he was talking to the jeweler about his watch, this cute girl who works there came over and said they'd just gotten in a brand-new pair of gold and pearl earrings and asked me if I would like to see them. So, just for fun, I went over to her counter and tried on the most beautiful set of earrings you have ever seen. I told her I loved them and asked how much they were. When she told me the price, I almost fainted on the spot and handed them right back, pronto.

And then to my surprise:

I don't know why it has taken me a long time to let go of even the smallest things, but yesterday morning I was finally gathering up some of Wilbur's old clothes to give to the Salvation Army. I was busy cleaning out his sock drawer, when I discovered a little black velvet box hidden in one of the socks. I opened it, and did I get a surprise. Inside the box was the same pair of gold and pearl earrings I had tried on last summer, along with a little note that said "Merry Christmas, Love, Wilbur."

I called the jewelry store, and they told me that Wilbur had put that girl up to letting me try on those earrings, so he could be sure I liked them before he bought them. Needless to say, I will treasure them forever, not because they are pretty—they are—but because they are from my Wilbur.

Merry Christmas,
Dot

Breaking a Heart

RUTHIE DIDN'T WANT to tell her father the bad news over the phone, so when she went back to Atlanta, she made a date to pick him up. When she pulled up to Briarwood, Mr. Merris was just walking out and unfortunately spotted her.

"Oh, hello, Mrs. Caldwell. Here to see your father?"

"Yes, Mr. Merris, I'm taking him to lunch."

"Oh, how nice. Well, we sure will miss him when he leaves, but he's told everybody all about his brand-new house, so I'm sure he'll be very happy."

Ruthie's heart sank. She'd hoped he hadn't said anything yet, but knowing Daddy and how excited he had been, she was not surprised. However, it sure was going to make telling him the news much harder.

LATER, AT LUNCH, after she had explained to him what had happened, and that rebuilding Whistle Stop was no longer a possibility, she could see he was terribly disappointed. But, true to form, he was more concerned about her. He said, "I hate that this happened, after all the hard work you gals put in. What do you think you'll do now?"

"I don't know yet, Daddy. But will you be all right? I wanted to do this for you so much, and now I can't."

"I know you did, honey. You tried your best. But sometimes things just don't go your way. And don't you worry one minute about me, sweetheart. I'm gonna be just fine."

"Really, Daddy?"

"Absolutely. Scout's honor."

BACK IN HIS little apartment that afternoon, Bud began to slowly unpack the things he'd started boxing up for his move to Whistle Stop. It had been such a lovely dream that now wasn't going to come true. And all because of a stupid piece of land. Poor little Ruthie. And poor him. Tomorrow he was going to have to tell Merris that he wouldn't be leaving Briarwood after all. That was not going to be pleasant. Particularly after he'd shot his big mouth off about how his daughter was redoing an entire town for him.

Back Where She Started

RUTHIE HAD NEVER been very comfortable with stark reality. She had always hated having to face cold, hard facts. In this case, the fact was that the project was not going to happen.

AFTER SHE BROKE the news to her father, Ruthie went back to her house on Caldwell Circle and sat down and had a good cry. She had hoped to have a little more time, but the real estate agent had called and informed her that the Vaughans, who had bought her house, had requested a thirty-day escrow so they could move in as soon as possible. She now had a house full of furniture and a lifetime of memories to pack. She'd planned to send everything to Whistle Stop. But now she had no place to put everything, or herself for that matter. Sweet Evelyn had wanted her to stay on at her guesthouse until she could find another project, but Ruthie couldn't impose on her. And if she wasn't working, what was the point of staying? She needed to come back and be close to her father.

CAROLYN WAS STILL upset with her about her selling her house, and Ruthie dreaded having to tell her that the project in Whistle

Stop was now off. When she arrived back in Atlanta, all Martha Lee had said was, "Well, look what the cat just drug in." Maybe she *had* been too hasty in selling her house. She should have just stayed where she was. All her big plans had gone up in smoke, and she was right back where she'd started. Only now she didn't have a place to live.

The very last thing on earth she wanted to do now was to look for an apartment and move all her things into some cold, impersonal storage bin. But that's just what she had to do. The following weeks were busy from morning to night, packing up the house and trying to find a decent place to rent. And at the end of each day she'd be exhausted. She soon began to wonder if she shouldn't just throw in the towel and go ahead and move into Briarwood herself. It was a bit early she knew, but she was probably going to wind up there anyway. Why wait?

The End of an Era

PEGGY WAS IN the back room of the clinic when she heard her cellphone tweet.

She looked and saw an email from Opal Butts in Birmingham. After she read it, she said to Bud, "Oh, honey, it's from Opal. Dot Weems died."

Bud had been looking at X-rays and turned to her.

"Oh no, what happened?"

"Opal said she had a stroke."

"Oh God, I hate to hear that. How old was she?"

"I'm sure she was in her early nineties, at least."

"She'd have to be. Or maybe older. She was a grown woman when we were little." Bud sighed. "My gosh. Dot Weems is gone. It's hard to believe. Well, it's certainly the end of an era."

Peggy said, "I agree, and now with Grady and Gladys Kilgore both gone, too, pretty soon we're going to run out of people who knew us when."

Dot Weems had lived to be 101, and was still volunteering at the Fairhope Library three days a week until the day she died. She would be missed. It was a long life, and one that had kept so many people connected.

The Dead Body

Two little ratty-looking twelve-year-old Gate City boys named Cooter and Lucas were up to no good this morning. They'd been over at the trailer park and had just raided Cooter's big brother's marijuana stash. They'd quickly stuffed it in their pockets, jumped on their bikes, took off, and rode out of town as fast as they could. The big brother had been to jail once and was mean. They knew if he caught them he would beat the living hell out of them.

After they had ridden far enough away, they pulled off the side of the road, hid their bikes behind some bushes, and walked down into the woods. Once they felt it was safe, they found a small clearing, sat down behind a tree, and emptied everything out of their pockets. They'd come away with at least ten hand-rolled marijuana cigarettes, a lighter, and three plastic bags of pills.

The bigger one, Cooter, who thought he was a tough guy, said, "Hot damn. I'm gonna smoke me two of these cigarettes and maybe three." But Lucas was nervous and kept looking around. "You don't reckon your brother saw us and followed us out here, do you?"

"Naw. Sling me over that lighter." Lucas threw the red plastic lighter over to Cooter, and it landed just behind him. When Cooter reached back to get it, he noticed something white sticking up in the leaves. As he looked closer, he suddenly jumped up. "Jesus Christ . . . it's a damn arm! Oh, shit, there's a goddamn dead body here! Let's get out of here!" And they both took off running as fast as they could. When they reached the road, they were both out of breath and white as sheets. They waved their arms and flagged down the next car that came down the road. When it stopped, they ran over to the driver and said, "There's a dead body down there, mister! We just found a dead body!"

The car's driver called 911.

THAT AFTERNOON, LIEUTENANT Geena Hornbeck walked into the snack room at the fire station and found two friends of hers from Search and Rescue sitting at the table laughing about something.

"What's so funny, guys?"

"Oh, Geena, you missed all the fun. This morning me and Harry got an emergency call, and when we got out to the location, these two skinny kids came running up to us screaming and hollering that they'd just found a dead body, that someone had been murdered and chopped up into pieces. They said there were arms and legs and blood everywhere. One kid was so scared he'd peed his pants."

Geena said, "Was there a dead body?"

"Wait, this is what's so funny. So we go down there to where they said the body was, and we see what they'd found. It was some old false arm somebody had thrown down there, laying under a tree."

"No . . ."

"Yeah, anyhow we dug all around real good to see if there was anything else down there, but we didn't find anything but some dope the kids left, and an old mason jar with some papers inside."

"Where was this?" asked Geena

"Out toward Gate City, down below the tracks. Maybe somebody threw it off the train, or something. I don't know. How in the hell do you lose a false arm?"

Geena said, "Guys, you're not going to believe this, but I happen to know somebody who lost his prosthetic arm a couple years ago. And it sounds like it was about in the same location."

The two guys were surprised. "You're kidding."

"No, my husband met him on the train. We even went to visit him at the hospital. Do you still have the arm?"

"Yeah, it's still out there on the table. Do you remember the man's name?"

"Yes, his name is Bud Threadgoode, and he lives over in Atlanta."

"Threadgoode?" Harry looked at his friend and said, "Wasn't that the name on that paper we found in the jar?"

"Yes. But it wasn't Bud Threadgoode. It was a woman's name, like Irene or something like that."

Geena was curious. "What kind of paper was it?"

"Some old land deed from the thirties. Maybe he had been carrying it with him at the time, who knows?"

"Do you still have it?"

"No. The chief said it looked pretty official, so he sent it over to the records department at the courthouse."

Geena said, "Oh. Okay. But in the meantime, I'll try and hunt down his phone number and let him know that we found his arm. I can't wait to tell Billy. He's not going to believe it."

. . .

AFTER GEENA LEFT the room, Harry said, "All I can say is this Threadgoode guy must be one strange dude, losing an entire arm and carrying his family papers around in a mason jar."

"You're still new on the job. Stick around. Last year, I had to get a guy off the top of a tree who thought he was an eagle. You ain't seen nothing yet. There's a lot of wackos out there."

Good News

RUTHIE WAS OVER in Atlanta when her cellphone rang. The call was from Birmingham but it wasn't Evelyn's number.

She picked up. "Hello?"

"Mrs. Caldwell, this is Jim Carder, and I'm calling with what I hope is some good news. I haven't been able to reach Mrs. Couch as yet, but I just received a call from the county courthouse, and they have somehow just located a deed that states the name of the owner of that tract of land. And it isn't Ligget."

"What?"

"No, it was a quitclaim deed that was signed over to another party on August 11, 1935. It was signed over to a Miss Imogene Threadgoode, now deceased, so if we can negotiate a sale or an easement with her heirs, we might be able to pull the project off after all. Isn't that great news?"

Ruthie was stunned. "You have no idea just how great."

"So we'll have to try and locate the current owner."

"Mr. Carder, the current owner, Mr. James Threadgoode, Jr., happens to be my father, and he's sitting across the table from me right now."

LATER, JIM FAXED them a copy of the deed, and Bud looked at it and said, "That's Aunt Idgie's signature, all right."

It had been witnessed, dated, and notarized, so it was legal. Of course, Bud had to produce Idgie's will naming him as her sole heir, and Jim took that down to the Jefferson County Hall of Records. A few weeks later, an official transfer of the property named James Threadgoode, Jr., as the land's owner, and it was he who now granted the necessary easements to Couch Properties, LLC. On that happy day, Bud handed the documents over to Ruthie and said, "Here you go, baby. Go and have yourself a ball."

A week later, his friend Billy's wife, Geena, the fire-person, had located his number and called to tell him that two of her co-workers had found his arm, along with a mason jar with a deed that had the name Threadgoode on it. She said, "I have your arm, but they sent the deed to the courthouse."

"Yes, I know," he said. "They sent that over to me last week. But, Geena, what I want to know is, where did they find that mason jar?"

She told him they'd been digging around and it had been buried under the same tree where they'd found his arm.

Bud had no idea that land had belonged to Aunt Idgie, or even more mysterious, why in the world she had buried the deed in a mason jar. But she had. And just when Ruthie needed it the most, somebody had found it.

That night when he was in bed, Bud couldn't help but wonder just what had guided him to that *particular* tree that day. There were hundreds of trees along the track—why that one? Had it been Idgie? If he hadn't left his arm there, the chances of anybody ever finding that jar would have been one in a million. No, more like one in a billion. It couldn't have been just a coincidence. After thinking more about it, Bud was convinced that it had to have been Aunt Idgie's doing. Crazy things like that just didn't happen in real life. Idgie had loved Ruthie and she obviously wanted Ruthie to have that cafe, and she had made damn sure that she got it.

After all these years, Aunt Idgie was still looking out for them. Bud decided he wouldn't tell anybody about her guiding him to that particular tree. He'd keep it their little secret.

An Old Acquaintance

IDGIE DIDN'T REMEMBER how she'd wound up in the back room of the River Club at two A.M. Eva Bates had tried to stop her from getting into a game with him, but the man had dared her. The two of them had somewhat of a history. And now, years later, he still had the little marks in his face as a reminder of when she'd shot him with a full load of buckshot that night he'd been trying to kill her cat. Arvel Ligget had waited a long time to catch Idgie Thread-goode outside of town.

Arvel was hard to look at, and even harder to like. The Depression had hit Alabama hard. People were so bad off, the saying went, that they got married just for the rice. And Arvel Ligget was good at taking advantage of people down on their luck. He ran a fly-by-night loan-shark outfit over in Pell City, and a lot of people were in debt to him. He was also good at cards. Most people around the area didn't have cash money to bet, and Arvel had won houses, land, and entire farms off of desperate men who had thought they could beat him at the poker table; poor men, with families, that had nowhere to go. But he didn't care. When they didn't vacate, he'd have them thrown out by a few of his henchmen.

Arvel had been determined to get even with Idgie, so when he saw her, sitting at the bar down at the River Club, he knew this was his chance. He dared her to go into the back room for a game of cards. At first she told him she didn't want to, but he'd goaded her. "I just dared you. . . . Are you scared to play with a real man?" Idgie rarely turned down a dare when she was sober, much less drunk and mad. Before she knew it, she was in the back room.

And now, after an hour at the poker table with Arvel, Idgie was on the verge of losing everything she had. Her friend Eva Bates was worried to death, and looked over at her daddy for help. But there wasn't a thing Big Jack Bates could do about it. He ran a clean game, and Ligget had just won the last hand, fair and square.

Idgie was suddenly in big trouble. She had just lost her car and her watch, and was now in to Arvel for five hundred dollars. Money that she and Ruth did not have.

Idgie wrote out her IOU for the five hundred, and said, "I'm done. You cleaned me out."

Arvel was disappointed. "Aw, you can't quit now. Let's play just one more game."

"You cleaned me out. I don't have anything left to bet." Idgie pushed back her chair and started to stand up.

Ligget said, "Now, wait. I hate to see you go home empty-handed. I'll tell you what. I'll give you a chance to win it all back, and I'll even sweeten the pot. Everything you owe me, plus there's twenty acres of land over in Whistle Stop I won awhile back. Come on. One game. Five card stud. Winner takes all."

Idgie said, "I told you once, Arvel. I don't have anything left to bet."

Arvel smiled. "Yeah, you do."

"What?"

"You've still got that cafe, don't you?"

Idgie shook her head. "No. I can't bet the cafe. My daddy gave me that."

"Your daddy's dead. And if I don't get the five hundred you owe me within three days, I'm gonna get that cafe anyway, so you might as well take a chance. Or are you too chicken?"

He had a point. Idgie had no idea where she was going to get five hundred dollars.

Arvel sat across the table rolling poker chips around in his hand, grinning at her and quietly clucking like a chicken. "Just think, Miss Idgie. You might get lucky. And that's a mighty fine piece of land."

"But I can't bet the cafe. Half of it belongs to Ruth. I can't take a chance on losing it."

"Why not? If you lose, that pretty little partner of yours can always pick up a little money on the side. I know a lot of men that would pay for a piece of that sweet-lookin' pie."

Idgie's eyes suddenly flashed with anger. "You lousy son of a bitch. I wish I had killed you when I had the chance."

He laughed. "But you didn't. And when I do get that cafe, you know what I'm gonna do? I'm gonna burn it down. You Thread-goodes think you're so high-and-mighty."

Idgie felt her entire face and ears burn red with rage. "God-damn you, Arvel. Deal the goddamn cards!"

Eva Bates let out a wail from over in the corner. Then she looked at Arvel and pleaded, "You know she don't mean it. She's drunk on her ass. Let her get on home."

Arvel said, "Too late. She said deal."

Eva looked at her daddy, but again, there was nothing he could do to stop it. The game was on. Big Jack walked over and stood by the table, watching Arvel to make sure he didn't try to pull some-thing. Eva was wringing her hands and said, "Oh Lordy, I'm so nervous my ears is ringin'."

After Idgie cut the deck, Arvel dealt her first card. She lifted up the corner and looked at it. Jack of clubs. A face card was a good start. Her next card was the eight of spades. Idgie was holding her breath and thinking, "Please let the next one be a jack." No luck, it was a four of hearts. Then her fourth and next to last card shot across the table. Two of spades. No help at all.

Fear must have sobered Idgie up because she could feel her heart pounding in her chest, and her palms were sweating.

Arvel threw her last card across the table. Idgie took a deep breath and looked. Eight of diamonds. She had nothing but a pair of eights.

Arvel glanced at his hand again, smiled, and threw in another chip. "I'll raise you another five hundred," and waited for Idgie to either fold or call.

Idgie knew he could be bluffing . . . or maybe not. If she folded now, she wouldn't get into more debt than she already was, but he would get the cafe. It would mean the end of everything she and Ruth had worked for.

The room was suddenly so quiet they could hear the clock ticking in the next room.

Finally Idgie said, "I'll see you, and raise you another five hundred," and threw in another chip.

Arvel looked surprised. But he threw in his chip and seemed happy to do so.

Big Jack said, "All right, Ligget. Show your hand." Arvel kept smiling as he laid out his cards one by one, and said, "Read 'em and weep. A pair of sevens, high card, ace of spades." He reached across the table to pull in his chips.

Big Jack said, "Wait a minute, Ligget. What do you have, Idgie?"

Idgie showed her hand, and Big Jack said, "The eights, jack high takes it."

Ligget's eyes narrowed. He wasn't used to losing. He said,

"Let's go again. I'll throw in another five hundred. And I've got a nice little farm I'll put up."

Big Jack shook his head. "Nope, that's it for the night, Arvel. I'm closing down the game. Now pay her what you owe her. I gotta go home."

A sulky Arvel counted out the cash and threw it at her, along with her car keys.

Big Jack said, "And we're gonna need the deed to that twenty acres of land she won."

"I ain't got it on me. I'll get it over to her later."

"Naw, you won't. Eva, run and get me one of them quitclaim deed documents and my notary stamp. You're gonna sign that land over to her tonight, and you ain't leaving here till you do."

Ligget thought about not signing it, but because of the nature of his business, Big Jack always carried a gun on his hip. He'd never had to pull it much, but he would. He just stood there looking at Arvel, gently resting his hand on the handle. Arvel got the message and signed the quitclaim deed over to Idgie. After he signed, Big Jack dated it, stamped it, and handed it to her. "Here you go, Idgie." Big Jack then said, "Eva, why don't you follow Idgie on home, make sure she gets there safe and sound."

The next morning, Idgie woke up still in her clothes, suddenly remembered what had happened, and broke out into a cold sweat. If Ruth ever found out what she had done—that she had taken a stupid chance on losing everything they owned, everything they had worked for all those years—she would probably never see Ruth or Buddy again. She realized she had to figure out a way to get rid of the evidence fast. She could have her brother Cleo hold the money she'd won, that was no problem. She didn't care about the stupid land. It was located way across the tracks and wasn't worth a thin dime. But she didn't want that bastard Ligget to have it, either, so she'd have to hide that deed and hide it good. She didn't trust that Ligget wouldn't try to steal it back. But more important at the moment was Ruth. If Ruth ever laid eyes on that deed with Idgie's signature on it, and saw the date she'd signed it, she would know exactly where she had been, what she had been doing, and when. Idgie knew she wouldn't be able to lie her way out of this one. That thought scared the hell out of her. She quickly got up out of bed, ran to the shed in the backyard, grabbed a shovel and an empty mason jar, and jumped in the car. With her head throbbing and feeling sick as a dog, she drove out past Double Springs Lake and parked. She walked across the meadow with her shovel and mason jar to the same tree where she always got her honey. Once she got there, with her head still throbbing, she started digging a hole at the base of the tree. As she dug, she could feel the hot morning sun hitting her back and the sweat running down her face, while hundreds of bees buzzed all around her. When she thought the hole was deep enough, she stuck the deed inside the mason jar, closed the lid tight, and buried it where she knew nobody would ever find it. Especially Ruth. Ruth was deathly afraid of bees.

Driving back home to the cafe that morning, still sick and shaky, Idgie vowed that from that day forward, she would give up gambling forever. And she did. Idgie never went to the River Club again. Except to get Buddy's dog. But she hadn't gone inside. Just up on the porch.

Buddy and Ruth would never know it, but almost half of his college tuition had been paid for by that one lucky poker game. And as for Arvel Ligget, a few months after Idgie beat him at that game of poker, his luck ran out again, and this time for good. He should have known that gambling with real money wasn't a safe thing to do. Too many men knew that, before he went home after a game, Ligget had a habit of stuffing his winning cash into his right sock. Not too many people had been surprised when his dead body was found out in the woods, barefooted and with an ice pick stuck in his neck.

Some said that it had been his own cousin that had done him in. The Liggets were never known to be a close-knit family. Not where money was concerned.

Ready to Begin Again

WHISTLE STOP, ALABAMA

WHEN THE EASEMENT documents came through, Evelyn called Ruthie immediately. "How soon can you get back over here?"

"I'm packing as we speak. Would three hours be soon enough?"

THE NEW ROADS leading in and out of town were being built, and new curbs and sidewalks put in. Utilities lines had been laid, and, after a lot of hard work on the part of the building crew, the cafe was finally almost finished. Evelyn and Ruthie had created an exact replica of Whistle Stop, only better. Unlike in the old cafe, everything in the kitchen now worked perfectly, plus, it had air-conditioning. The living quarters in the back were just about ready for Ruthie to move into. She wanted to live onsite, so she could oversee the rest of the work.

As the project progressed, Evelyn Couch, who was on the board of a local theater group, called her friends Philip and Bruce, who were set decorators, to come work on the project. Ruthie explained to them what she needed, and, using all the old photos of the town, they went to work. Philip found a photograph of the old Whistle Stop railroad crossing sign, created a new one, and put it back where the old one had been. They also re-created the original cafe signs and the old green lettering on the windows that read

FRIED GREEN TOMATOES. They had even copied the old original cafe menus from the thirties. Only the prices were changed. Who could serve a full breakfast these days for twenty-five cents?

BUD'S NEW HOUSE was coming along nicely. And at the old Threadgoode family home, pieces of rotten wood were replaced and painted. The lawn was replanted, and the old chinaberry tree in the front yard trimmed.

As they stood admiring it, Evelyn said, "You know what, Ruthie? This old house would make a perfect bed and breakfast. It has eight bedrooms and a big kitchen."

Ruthie agreed. "It would be perfect. I found some pictures of vintage rose-patterned wallpaper online. I can do the entire house over in the exact same period. It was built in 1894, so when you go in, you'll feel like you're going back in time. I'll bet people would love to stay here."

Evelyn looked at her and smiled. "Are we having fun or what?"

SEVERAL WEEKS LATER, Ruthie was busy overseeing the hanging of the deer head above the cafe counter when her cellphone rang. It was her dad.

"Hey, it's me. Honey, are you sitting down?"

Oh dear. She walked over and sat down. She could tell by the tone of his voice that something either terribly bad or terribly good must have happened.

"Yes, Daddy, what's up?"

"I just wanted you to be the first one to know that we eloped."

"You did what?"

"Lois and I got married at the courthouse down in Columbus."

"You and Lois ran off and got married?"

"Just to Columbus. We were back in time for lunch."

"Well, this is a surprise. Why didn't you tell me?"

"I would have, but I thought it might upset you . . . because of your mother."

"No, no. I'm happy for you, Daddy. I like Lois."

"Can we come over and visit? We have a car and a driver all lined up. I want her to see where we'll be living."

"Of course, Daddy."

"And can Virgil come, too?"

"Fine."

This was something Ruthie hadn't expected, but then why not? The more the merrier.

BRIARWOOD MANOR BEING such a social place, news naturally traveled fast. Over at Caldwell Circle, Martha Lee had just been called by a friend and informed of the latest excitement.

After she hung up, she looked as if she might faint. She turned to Gerta and exclaimed, "My God, Bud Threadgoode has just married the Coca-Cola heiress!"

Luckily, Gerta caught her right before she hit the ground.

The Chicks Return

ALTHOUGH THEY HAD tried to keep it quiet, an article about the renovation project appeared in *The Birmingham News*. But it turned out to be good news for Evelyn and Ruthie, who were now busy looking for people to hire for the grand opening.

Opal's granddaughter Bea, who was also a hairdresser, saw the article about the town of Whistle Stop opening back up. She quickly called the office and left a message. "Mrs. Couch, you don't know me, but my name is Bea Wallace, and my grandmother Opal Butts used to own the beauty shop in Whistle Stop. I was wondering if you had rented out that space yet. If not, I would love to talk to you about it."

Earlier in the day Alberta Peavey had called, telling her that she was an experienced chef and could bring her grandmother's recipes with her. That is, if there happened to be a job opening.

When Evelyn heard that she almost started to cry. Suddenly all the little chickens were coming home to roost.

And soon there would be another chicken flying in.

After hearing that the old Whistle Stop church had been restored, a young female minister fresh out of the seminary showed up at the office and expressed an interest in starting a new congregation. She explained that it would mean a lot to her, because her grandfather had once been the preacher there. She said her name was Jessie Jean Scroggins.

All they needed now was someone to run the new bed and breakfast.

It was Saturday, and Ruthie was busy on the Internet looking at wallpaper, when her phone rang. When she picked up, a somewhat familiar voice said, "Mrs. Caldwell?"

"Yes?"

"You may not remember me, but I was your father's nurse a few years ago when he was at UAB Hospital."

"Terry?"

"Yes. You remember me!"

"Well, of course I remember you. How are you?"

"Hanging in there. How's sweet ol' Bud doing, still sassy as ever?"

"Oh, sure, but what a surprise to hear from you. Are you still over at UAB Hospital?"

"No, I retired last year."

"Oh, really?"

"Yes, it was time, but listen, I know you're busy so I will get straight to the point. I've been reading a little bit in the papers about what you and Mrs. Couch are doing, and I read that you are looking for someone to run a bed and breakfast."

"Yes, we are."

"Now, this may be a complete long shot, but I was wondering if I might apply for the job."

"Oh, Terry, are you serious?"

"Yes, I've had a lot of experience looking after people, and believe it or not, I'm a hell of cook."

At that moment, Evelyn walked in the door and Ruthie said, "Hold on a minute, Terry," and she put her hand over the phone.

"Evelyn, it's Terry, Daddy's nurse from UAB calling."

"Oh yes. How is she?"

"She's retired from nursing and wants to know if she can apply for the B&B job."

Evelyn quickly walked over and took the phone. "Terry, this is Evelyn Couch. Why, hell yes, you can apply. Get yourself over here."

LATER, AFTER THEY gave Terry the job, Ruthie said, "Won't Daddy be pleased? He really liked Terry. And I think it's good to have an ex-nurse around, don't you?"

"Yes," Evelyn said. "And think about it, Ruthie. You'll be managing the cafe, Terry is running the B&B, Bea will have the beauty shop, plus with Alberta cooking and Jessie Jean preaching it's going to be an all-gal town. Your dad is going to be the only man here."

Ruthie smiled. "Knowing Daddy, he's sure to love that."

Look What the Cat Dragged In

WHISTLE STOP, ALABAMA

IT WAS IN the middle of one of those sudden Alabama rainstorms when she heard someone knocking loudly on the back door of the cafe. Ruthie opened it, and to her surprise, there stood Martha Lee Caldwell, soaked to the bone, with suitcase in hand.

"I have come to Alabama, not with a banjo on my knee, but to fling myself upon your mercy."

"Oh, Martha, come in. What happened? What are you doing here? Aren't you supposed to be at Briarwood?"

Martha Lee stepped inside. "I *was*, but I was told by that little worm Richard Merris that Briarwood had a waiting list and I'm number six. Can you believe it? Me? On a *waiting* list? He said my financials are not acceptable at the moment. Well, we'll see about that."

She then affected the best humble look she could manage and said, "Might you have some small little corner where I could wait? I promise I'll be as quiet as a mouse."

"Oh, of course you can. But my gosh, Martha, does Carolyn know? I'm sure she'd love to have you come stay with her."

Martha Lee looked at her strangely. "Haven't you heard?"

"No, heard what?"

"Carolyn is getting a divorce."

"What?"

"Yes. But I'll let her tell you the particulars, I must lie down now. I'm tired to the bone."

Of course, after that, Ruthie didn't sleep a wink all night.

The phone call came early the next morning.

"Mother, Brian has left me, and moved in with another woman."

"Oh, honey, what happened?"

"He left me for his dental hygienist. Can you imagine?"

"Oh, no."

"I am so humiliated I could just die. All our friends know. I can't stay here another minute."

"Does Grandmother know Brian moved out?"

"Yes. But I can't talk to her about it, she wouldn't understand. I need to be with you right now. Can Cameron and I come down there with you?"

"Of course you can, darling, and don't you worry. We'll figure something out, okay?"

"Oh, thank you, Mother, I don't know what I would do if I didn't have you to turn to."

After Ruthie hung up, she was heartbroken for her daughter, but also a little hopeful. It was the first time she had ever heard Carolyn say that she needed her. And that felt good. Life certainly had its twists and turns. Her daughter and her granddaughter would be coming to Whistle Stop to be with her. Maybe forever. Who knows? There was a brand-new school opening up not far from there. Ruthie had to stop herself from getting too far ahead of herself. But it was a possibility.

The Grand Opening

WHISTLE STOP CAFE
Present Day

EVERYBODY WAS THERE for the cafe's big grand opening. Ruthie's son, Richard, and his girlfriend, Dotsie, came all the way from Oregon and were delighted. Being vegan, they could eat all the fried green tomatoes they wanted. Bud and Lois were there, along with Billy Hornbeck and Geena. And many of the grandchildren of Reverend Scroggins and Sheriff Grady flew in from out of town. Janice Rodgers, a popular news anchor at the local TV station, came out and filmed a special feature on the town and cafe, and interviewed Bud about the old days. Later, the mayor of Birmingham dropped by and presented them with a plaque, declaring that July 28 would be forever proclaimed "Whistle Stop Day." All the railroad engineers had been alerted about the event, and every train that passed by blew its whistle in honor of the day.

Later, Bud and Lois walked to the cafe for lunch, and after Bud had eaten a full plate of fried green tomatoes, Alberta Peavey came out of the kitchen and asked, "How were they, Mr. Threadgoode?"

He looked up at her and smiled. "Alberta, my dear, let's put it this way. If I wasn't already married, I'd ask you to marry me on the spot. These are the best fried green tomatoes I've had since 1949."

It was one of those days that Bud would never forget. His whole family was back together again, and Whistle Stop was up and running once more.

Martha Lee, with her new business partner Carolyn, had opened an antique shop in the building where the post office used to be. They would feature fine Asian porcelains, of course. The new Busy Bea Beauty Shop was next door and doing very well.

And as for Evelyn Couch, she was extremely happy. As usual, after a rocky start, another one of her investments had paid off big-time. The woman couldn't lose for winning, and she enjoyed being back in the game. In fact, she was starting construction on thirty new two-story condo units that she was building behind the cafe called One Railroad Place. She was planning to market it to the younger set, with a top-of-the-line fitness center that would include a large indoor heated pool and a fresh juice and coffee bar. She was even thinking of moving there herself. Her house was too big for one person, and besides, as she found out, it's a good thing to have younger friends.

They say that timing is everything. As luck would have it, a few months after the cafe opened, Birmingham suddenly became a serious "foodie" town. With an exultant write-up in *The Birmingham News* and a great television review, almost overnight, the Whistle Stop Cafe became *the* trendy place to eat. A place that, as one food critic wrote, offered "Delightfully Delicious Authentic Farm-to-Table Cuisine."

Soon, they had customers coming from as far away as Atlanta and Nashville. It was such a success that they had to expand the cafe to almost triple its original size. Someone said that if Ruth and Idgie could have seen the place today, they wouldn't have believed it. Who would have dreamed that Sipsey's fried green tomatoes would ever be considered gourmet food, or that the

Whistle Stop Cafe would be taking lunch and dinner reservations weeks in advance?

And here's something else Ruthie would never have guessed. Since the cafe décor was green and white, it was amazing how cute those two hundred frogs looked on the shelves.

Epilogue

A YEAR AGO, Bud Threadgoode had given up on making plans for the future, but today, he and Lois were busy planning a world cruise.

It was hard for Ruthie to believe, but this morning her daddy was flying to Europe on a private jet with his new wife and Virgil. She had to laugh. At this point, Virgil had traveled to more places than she had. But then, she hadn't married the Coca-Cola heiress. Before Bud left he called her from the airport and said, "Ruthie, don't forget what I told you, to enjoy every minute. That's what Lois and I are doing."

And as it so happened, so was she. She loved waking up every morning, going to work at the cafe, meeting and greeting people from all over the country, serving them good food, and telling them the story of Idgie and Ruth. Just last week they had an entire busload of tourists come in for lunch.

But there was this one person in particular who had been coming in quite a bit lately. A nice-looking retired investment banker from Birmingham, a widower. Ruthie could tell he liked her, and she was surprised at how much that pleased her. A boyfriend at her age? Well, why not? Look at her daddy. He'd found love at eighty-nine. Her future was wide open with possibilities. Didn't they say sixty was the new forty? And he did remind her of Brooks. After being so down for so long, she just couldn't wait to see what tomorrow would bring.

Acknowledgments

I'd like to thank my agents, Jennifer Rudolph Walsh, Sylvie Rabineau, and Suzanne Gluck, and Random House Publishing for all their support throughout the years, with very special thanks to my longtime editor and friend, Kate Medina.

ABOUT THE AUTHOR

FANNIE FLAGG's career started in the fifth grade when she wrote, directed, and starred in her first play, titled *The Whoopee Girls*, and she has not stopped since. At age nineteen she began writing and producing television specials, and later wrote for and appeared on *Candid Camera*. She then went on to distinguish herself as an actress and a writer in television, films, and the theater. She is the bestselling author of *Daisy Fay and the Miracle Man*; *Fried Green Tomatoes at the Whistle Stop Cafe*; *Welcome to the World, Baby Girl!*; *Standing in the Rainbow*; *A Redbird Christmas*; *Can't Wait to Get to Heaven*; *I Still Dream About You*; *The All-Girl Filling Station's Last Reunion*; and *The Whole Town's Talking*. Flagg's script for the movie *Fried Green Tomatoes* was nominated for an Academy Award and the Writers Guild of America Award and won the highly regarded Scripter Award for best screenplay of the year. She is also the winner of the Harper Lee Prize. Fannie loves all animals, especially human beings, and lives happily in California and Alabama.

ABOUT THE TYPE

This book was set in Electra, a typeface designed for Linotype by W. A. Dwiggins, the renowned type designer (1880–1956). Electra is a fluid typeface, avoiding the contrasts of thick and thin strokes that are prevalent in most modern typefaces.